love at first sight

love at first sight

AN ALAN ZIEGLER READER

NL

NARRATIVE LIBRARY

Many of these pieces appeared in the following books and periodicals:

Planning Escape (Release Press); *So Much to Do* (Release Press); *The Green Grass of Flatbush* (Word Beat Press); *In the City of Mystery* (Pudding House Press); *The Swan Song of Vaudeville: Tales and Takes* (Zoo Press); *The Writing Workshop Note Book: Notes on Creating and Workshopping* (Soft Skull Press/Counterpoint); *The Apalachee Quarterly; Cavalier Literary Couture; Columbia* magazine; *Columbia Spectator; Connections; The International Literary Quarterly; Journal of a Living Experiment; Milk Quarterly; Narrative* Magazine; *The New Yorker;* the *New York Times; The Paris Review; The Party Train: A Collection of North American Prose Poetry; Second Coming; Street; Sun; Utne Reader*

Narrative Magazine, Inc., is a registered 501(c)(3) nonprofit organization.
NarrativeMagazine.com

Cover and book design by Miller360

Please direct any questions or comments to:
editors@narrativemagazine.com

For my sister and brother: Karen Luchen and Philip Ziegler

*

My deepest thanks to:

Lacy Crawford for constructing this book with fervor and acumen.

Tom Jenks for editorial wisdom and timely support.

Mimi Kusch for her attention to detail and nuance.

Eleanor Jackson for being the agent of my dreams.

And always, Erin.

contents

Introduction

Alan Ziegler's poetry deals in moments, the stuff of life. He calls his poems "tales" or "takes," making readers think of cinematography, possibly imagining the author sitting in the director's chair on set, rehearsing his scenes until they are just right. Like the "reality" conveyed in films, his writing has the effect of seeming off-the-cuff yet perfectly honed. Or like the improvised takes of a jazz musician, Ziegler's seem like spontaneous expressions—memorable but unrepeatable.

Great poets have written narrative poetry, and the more Ziegler's work brings those poets to mind, the more his own poems stand out. Robert Frost's *North of Boston* poems read like one-act plays—long dialogue-driven pieces mostly framed in the present tense. Set against these, Ziegler's poems are remarkable for their efficiency. His are anecdotal, economical, and mostly framed in the past tense. It makes sense that Ziegler developed his writing skills as a journalist. Throughout his childhood and college years, he wrote for school newspapers (his elementary school newspaper was devised as something to do for the five students who weren't deemed good enough to make the choir), and he secured a job as a journalist after he graduated from college. His takes are like brief clips of rare footage that capture the newsworthy, even the rapturous, amid the ordinary. These glimmers of life within our lives give us the fleeting sense that something significant has happened. The more nameless that something is, the more significant it seems.

Many of Ziegler's scenes, whether depicted in prose or poetry, illustrate the connection between individuals, even as they are necessarily separated. In "Late One Night," Ziegler writes about perceived connections between ourselves and strangers. This same theme preoccupied Walt Whitman in *Leaves of Grass:*

> The machinist rolls up his sleeves, the policeman travels
> his beat,
> the gate-keeper marks who pass,
> The young fellow drives the express-wagon, (I love him
> though I do not know him;)

But Whitman's celebrations are different from Ziegler's. Ziegler is interested in paradoxes: How is it that anyone can feel alone on New York City's crowded sidewalks? There is loneliness in crowds but also a kind of companionship that will do in a pinch. Everyone is at least connected by their isolation in common. For Ziegler there is a real possibility of connection through empathy, the recognition of our own isolation in others. (Don't miss the story "Lonely" in the pages that follow.)

The problem of our isolation bears especially on romantic relationships. Ziegler's tales often illustrate the fusion (and confusion) of identities that happens when two people become a couple. The unity of a couple can be confusing, but determining what individuality remains for each partner can be more confusing. In "Swan," the speaker has learned that just as everyone desires companionship, so do they desire "space." But the most disconcerting theme in Ziegler's writing isn't our isolation from others but our strangeness to ourselves:

> She made him beside himself, and he hardly recognized the man standing next to him.

Though Ziegler's poems are full of human troubles, they are far from pessimistic. Ziegler finds comedy in our isolation, in the absurd incompatibility between the genders, and in our missed connections and miscommunications. His takes are optimistic—and ultimately cathartic—in much the same way as blues music. He handles his concerns with levity and wit:

> She put her finger on his wrist but couldn't find a pulse. They disagreed on the implications.

His humor ranges from subtle to slapstick, and sometimes it's both at once. In "Love Potions and Bitter Pills," the speaker grasps at straws to find the words that will salvage his relationship and comes up with, "It's you and me against the world, babe." She gets the upper hand, coming back with the witty rejoinder, "You are the world to me." Ziegler doesn't sugarcoat difficult truths with humor; the truths themselves are humorous, and the wit in the stories offers encouragement and consolation.

Ziegler's pieces on teaching writing are similarly encouraging. For almost thirty years, he's been a roaming writer in residence and a professor of writing and pedagogy at Columbia University, helping shape the university's approach to the teaching of creative writing. (He is the first professor of the arts to receive Columbia's Presidential Award for Teaching.) He has contributed three books to the field.

Ziegler fell into teaching when asked to substitute in a writers-in-the-schools program at a Brooklyn elementary school. He notes, "I didn't plan to be a teacher of creative writing any more than I planned to be a creative writer." His attribution of achievement to providence is a mark of his modesty, but it's also central to the guiding spirit of his work, both in the classroom and on the page: the embrace of incidence. Intention always takes a backseat to occasion. Once, on a New York City street, a madman ran up to Ziegler: "Do you know what happened?" he asked.

"Where?" replied Ziegler.

"Anywhere!" said the madman, and ran off.

This is Ziegler's parable of writing. For him, the intrusive nature of the message and the grubbiness of the messenger make the commandment all the more compelling: Pay attention! This dictum reveals the internal logic of Ziegler's prose and poetry alike.

Ziegler's observations, re-created in his writings, make an argument for the pathos and heartbreak of our relationships with those we pass on the sidewalk or see regularly but know only as silhouettes in a window. His form and manner are uniquely original, yet his preoccupations and themes are distinctly American. Resonances of Frost, Whitman, Edward Hopper, and contemporary musicians such as Joni Mitchell are occasionally perceptible, like the fleeting moments of recognition in the eyes of strangers in subway cars.

This book is arranged in near-chronological order, beginning with poems and stories from Ziegler's four collections, which were published between 1973 and 2004. That work is highlighted by an excerpt from Ziegler's 1977 essay "Pausing and Looking Back," in which he considers his experience teaching poetry in New York City public schools. The excerpt simultaneously serves as an introduction to several notes drawn from *The Writing Workshop Note Book,* a compendium of dispatches from Ziegler's desk regarding creation, frustration, and inspiration, designed for the student writer (or any writer willing to consider herself still learning). Finally, this book includes several sections from Ziegler's memoir, *Based on a True Life: A Memoir in Pieces.*

Written in short prose poems, *Based on a True Life* gathers force through a careful juxtaposition of intimate character-based pieces. In the edited selection here we have endeavored to create a narrative that accurately represents the complete work. At the end of our selection we've placed "Father Stories: Observation Deck," in which Ziegler's taciturn father reveals his secret life growing up with gangsters, as he and Alan watch a sunset from the roof of the Empire State Building. In telling the tale, Ziegler lends his poetic magic to open out his father's reluctant speech.

But even this bit of illumination is an inside joke. His father's revelations notwithstanding, Ziegler doesn't believe that art is born of the lightning strike but of inspired determination. It's a democratic approach to art, and it enables him to awaken poetry in students who might ordinarily scoff at working at a desk. Ziegler teaches careful observation, steady wonder, humorous reflection, and regular tinkering. The tools of love, and of life itself.

—*Narrative* Editors
San Francisco
May 2011

from
Planning Escape

Things to Do Today

This is a report
on the shape of the commune
at the present time:
The dishes need to be washed
and the candle on the kitchen table
is almost burnt out; the laundry
that has just been washed
needs to be folded and put away;
it's stuffy, the windows need to be
opened, and Nancy, looking sad,
needs to be talked to
before she leaves for the weekend.

Treatment

One day with no warning
the music stops—
there is something wrong
with your stereo and you
don't know if it's a minor
adjustment or a major breakdown
but you do nothing about it
and go music-less for months till
someone moves in and says
hey I'll take it down to the shop
don't worry I'll pay,
but you say no
I can fix it myself
and you do.

Sacrifice

as i'm trying to close the jammed
window, it slips and
slams on my finger.
i cannot re-open it.
you are in the other room.
i call your name calmly
so as not to alarm you.
after a while you say,
"what do you want?"
gently i say,
"please come here."
by now there is no pain
in my trapped finger.
a minute later
you come strolling into the room
as i think
of the many ways
i am good to you.

Trial

after you said
you were leaving,
I took off the ring
I'd been wearing for years
and put it away
to see if I could get used to
the feel of nothing
but my own skin

Soon

like a dream gone haywire
you lifted yourself
out of my sleep

i am still sluggish

when i am fully awake
i will call for you

this time we will
not live as if
in a car

i will be able to speak
to you without
feeling like i am
biting into glass

Too Late
(after Berryman)

A baseball cap,
team's emblem
crookedly sewn on,
lies boyless
on the railroad track
like a stranded puppy.
The boy knows
no other emblem can
be sewn so precisely
crooked
on another cap.
He is driven to it
by tears, held back
by mother,
his desire so pure
I would have to
unravel my memory
to find it in me.
I would risk my life
for that cap.
But it is 2 a.m.
There is no boy around.
And the trains
stopped running
years ago.

The River

on one side of the river
is a family
where i sit quietly at dinner
surrounded by chatter
they are polite to me
and my work
they use their knives
only to cut meat

while on the other side
the knives are used
at the wrong move
of a hand or mouth
and if you break a silence
you better have
a damn good reason

from the bridge
i look down at the water
where the fish
know their boundaries

Accident

There was a tree
in the middle of the road.
I swerved
to avoid it and went
crashing
into 500
miles of open space.
I've never been the same.

from
So Much to Do

So Much to Do

Could you come over here? There are a few things I want to go over. For example, your naked arms.

Particularly above the elbows. I don't see much of your arms now that the weather is cold. Not that they are never there for me, but I have been conditioned to focus along the center of your bare body and slightly to the left and right. At some of the best moments your arms are completely out of sight, around me, drawing me closer to your face. Ah, your face, I could spend hours there, but not right now. Above the elbows, the backs of your knees, your ankles, your softly curved calves—especially your calves, I want to wrap around them the way the tops of your socks do. Also, the back of your neck (one of the most underrated parts of the body), a kiss there just hard enough not to tickle. I want so much of you, dream-volumes of flesh, hair, nails. The third rib from the bottom on the left side, I've been meaning to get there for six weeks. All the neglected outskirts, acquaintances on the peripheries of the intimate friendships I have formed with the flashier parts of your body. Those special friends will not be jealous, they will understand why I pass them over—indeed, they will share in the good fortunes of their neighbors. And they know I will return home before I sleep.

Going Out to Eat Alone

It is suddenly spring and you are in Michigan, where names like Leelanau, Leland, and the Grand Traverse Bay have replaced Manhattan, West End, and the Hudson River. I go back inside and shed the layer of down I have grown this winter, replacing it with the jacket I haven't worn since you borrowed it in September. Walking along the river, I dive my hands into the jacket pockets, instinctively hunching against the wind. But the wind has dwindled into a breeze. Crumpled paper snuggles between my fingers. I lift it out, wondering if it is an important note from way back: a telephone number I was supposed to call, or a reminder to meet someone (who is just now thawing out on the street corner).

A gum wrapper. I haven't chewed gum in years. I smile as I picture you walking along the bay, chewing gum. A crumpled gum wrapper on my way to a table-for-one: the kind of discovery that would make this a sad poem, if you weren't coming back.

Love at First Sight

It was a novelty store and I went in just for the novelty of it. She was in front of the counter, listening to the old proprietor say: "I have here one of those illusion paintings, a rare one. You either see a beautiful couple making love, or a skull. They say this one was used by Freud himself on his patients—if at first sight you see the couple, then you're a lover of life and love. But if you focus on the skull first, you're closely involved with death, and there's not much hope for you."

With that, he unwrapped the painting. She and I hesitated, then looked at the picture, then at each other. We both saw the skull. And have been together ever since.

Ties

I'm not sure what to say when the man comes to my door and mumbles something about being my brother. It is true that I do have a brother, but this man does not resemble him. The man is battered, with traces of blood on his face. What to say to him? After all, I would not want to reject him and find out later that he really is my brother, that he had been marred beyond recognition in a war or accident, had plastic surgery, and was recently reinjured. But if he is not my brother, he must be someone who no longer knows who he is, someone going from door to door hoping finally to reach the right door, where his true brother waits anxiously. I do not want to impede this journey by taking him in as my own brother, thus keeping him from finding his real identity. And what if I take him in and someday my real brother shows up in need, what do I do then? There is only so much room in this small house.

At this moment my wife comes home and instantly recognizes the man as her brother. So, he has been in the right place all along. Suddenly the house seems even smaller than before, and I wonder if it can hold three. I fear there may not be enough room for me. I hope there is space at my brother's.

Neighbor

At 12:44 p.m.
on a hungover Sunday
I eat breakfast
while across the way
an opera singer blasts
through her warm-ups.
I sort out my life,
trying to determine
if it's come down to:
"How nice to be in New York,
within ear's touch
of a stranger's art,"
or:
"Hey, lady,
take it someplace else."

Swan

As I was walking
a swan came out of the river.
I told her all about you,
pointing to where you lay in the sun,
facing us with your eyes closed,
pink sweater on the grass.
She started toward you.
I told her you wanted to be left alone.
She turned and eased back down into the river.
Why, she hardly knew you—
and understood so quickly
it put me to shame.

Taking the Offensive

I want to overthrow
the government of your silence,
rebel against the tyranny
of your unwillingness,
sabotage your repression.

I aim to shake things up.

Don't talk to me about moderation.
I've tried going through channels.
Don't tell me to have patience,
I've done it all, and slowly:
I wrote letters,
appealed to your better senses,
petitioned for access to your heart,
and lay vigil by your side many a night.

I am as sorry as you are
it has come to this,
for I am a reasonable man
who has swallowed more than his share
of reasons.

I will start with brief incursions,
then escalate.
Please don't let it get to terrorism.

I know that will crumble
the good with the bad.

Don't take this as a threat
and bolster your defenses.
Take it as an invitation:
Join me.

I think, under it all,
we both want the same thing.
I seek a new order.

On the Road

That winter the news spread fast through the suburban high
   school:
Barry Brown has run away.
First he didn't show up for school,
not too unusual, he'd slipped off to Greenwich Village
several times before, always back before panic.
But now it was two, three days, no word,
and his parents used the word *frantic* a lot.
At first we withheld judgment,
excited by the possibilities but also slightly worried,
though not frantic.
Then word started coming in—
someone spotted him in Times Square, outside of Playland,
but he ran when called;
someone else who hardly knew him said she got a phone call
from Texas he sounded real happy and was keeping a journal.
We started repeating things he'd said that fall,
schemes for "getting away from here" as his eyes glowed
during long nights of talk and beer in the field behind the
   school.

Our talks resumed without him,
in basements, cars, or around a fire on the deserted beach:
we'd all do what Barry did,
maybe this summer, before our senior year; maybe instead of
   college.

I remembered Barry whispering in my ear during an English
   exam,
"Read *On the Road*, it's the Bible,"
and the teacher accused us of cheating and Barry just
   laughed.
Summer came, we were still talking and I said damn we talk,
but Barry did it.
It was early in the morning but hot already when they found
   him
entangled in an unfinished sewer pipe.
As construction resumed after a bad winter then a long strike,
a worker screamed under the street
not more than two blocks from Barry's house.
They found Barry trapped in some stupid journey, unable to
   get very far
or back to where he came from.
His agony hit us all behind the eyes,
though we didn't talk much about it, saving it for moments
of private nightmare.
No one went anywhere that summer.
But eventually we all did.

Late One Night
(July, 1975)

Except for one query for "some coin" no one has bothered me
no one is bothering anyone around Sheridan Square
it is 3:30 a.m. and maybe everyone is too tired
maybe all the hustlers have either found what they wanted or
    given up
and those still out are there with interior not ulterior motives
nothing is harsh
except for the baldly lit all-night grocery store
it hurts my eyes to walk in there
I quickly grab an orange juice pay get out
a dozen or so are scattered around the Square
in twos, threes, and ones
no one is going anywhere
sunrise is a safe two hours away

Kathy is still cleaning up at the Lion's Head
the dining room is empty except for her
the last crowd is gathered at the bar
some will linger until four, no more are let in
Kathy looks so tired, and there's still more work to do
I can't help and can't bear to watch
so I go back outside
looking in store windows, feeling like I look like I'm available
though I'm not
but no one bothers me
I feel like I can even say hello to the woman passing me

without it being misunderstood
but I don't say anything, just stare at the window display

on the corner, they are talking about the horse who broke
    her leg today
I watched the match race with my father, read the early
    editions,
Foolish Pleasure vs. Ruffian, colt against mare,
the nation watching, wearing "He" and "She" buttons
they didn't know if they could save her
my father remembered when they used to shoot them right
    at the track
when he used to go with his father
I overhear someone say that Ruffian has been "put to sleep"
and it affects me
though not as much as Rod Serling and Tim Buckley
who also died recently
and who meant a lot to me
earlier Cliff called from Boston
to talk about Buckley, it was not only that he died at 28, a
    year older than us
but it reminded him how much has changed
since we used to listen to his music
or jammed with him at Newport in '68, the night before his
    performance
the Newport Folk Festival is gone,
the women we were with then are gone, have been for years
and Buckley had been driving a cab, though there was talk of
    a comeback
and Rod Serling—I tried to write a poem about him

how he'd influenced me more than many "great" writers
taught me irony and voice
in the poem I kicked myself for not having visited him
he was a college professor at the end and probably accessible
I ended the poem with: "you were 50 / younger than my
    father / and I can't imagine him / dying either"

but on the corner they are talking about the great filly, Ruffian
and I understand that loss, too, though I don't know much
    about horses
she was at the top of her game
but I sense her death means more than money to those who
    owned and followed her
I suppose they'll talk about this race
in future years when there are other match races on TV
how she broke down leading by a neck
how the colt went through the motions
gliding eerily to the finish alone, in front of 50,000 shocked
    fans
and I'll remember having seen it
perhaps even more vividly recall hearing them talk about it
on a peaceful night in Sheridan Square
and every so often friends and I will exchange "Twilight
    Zone" plots
and every so often we'll pull out Tim Buckley albums

I am now sitting in front of the Lion's Head
jotting some of this down
Kathy comes out the door, her work is done

I'm nervous because she has just spent time with an old
    boyfriend
but she smiles and leans against my body
and tells me that late this afternoon, while I was on Long
    Island
the city was flooded by rain, the subways stopped running
and she got caught in the downpour
I tell her it didn't even rain on Long Island
where I played ball with my kid brother before the race
and it didn't rain at nearby Belmont Racetrack, where Ruffian
    broke down
because, an expert said, the track might have been too hard
where the losing jockey was quoted—in separate articles—
as saying the horse's leg broke "like a stick" and "like a twig"
(I can't tell if it was the jockey or the reporters
who couldn't make the distinction)
and the jockey refused to look at films of the race right away

from Kathy's roof I can see the Albert Hotel, where once
I was supposed to visit Tim Buckley but didn't,
and I can see the sun began to rise.

from
The Green Grass of Flatbush

The Vassar Lecture

Do you want to hear something embarrassing?

When I was in high school, I told a girl who I was trying to make fall for me that the three ingredients necessary
for love are Magic, Mystery, and Motion: "The Three M's."
My romantic notion softened her eyes. I stared at her on
the doorstep, and when she expected me to kiss her, I said,
"Sometimes the most beautiful sounds a jazz musician makes
are the notes he doesn't play. I'll call you in the morning."

I still remember her captured look before I turned quickly
and left. When I reached the corner I was sure she was still
standing there, caught up in the mystery of the moment. I
turned, and there she was. I threw her a kiss. But some chemical change occurred during the night, and when morning
came the magic had gone. I didn't call her, and I avoided her
in school on Monday.

I cringe to think of incidents like that, but what good is
growing up if it doesn't make you cringe later? Although I
rarely use the words *magic, mystery, and motion,* I still treasure
them when they come along—with the possible exception
of mystery, which I've had about enough of. Nowadays,
"consistency" and "sustenance" come more easily to my
tongue, and are just as elusive as the Three M's.

Another concept that played a big part in my youthful
escapades with love was "proof." It was important to prove
you loved somebody, and for them to prove it back, with bold
gestures. For other guys, the girl could prove it with sex, as
in "Prove you love me, baby." For me that was too common,
too indelicate. Plus, I realized early in the game that girls like

it as much as boys do. Sex wasn't proof of anything more than a certain need for a certain time.

Proof could take the shape of showing up when the person least expected you. Like the time I had a screaming fight with a girlfriend. (I said we were lacking motion: "This relationship isn't *going* anywhere.") I told her I didn't want to see her anymore, and meant it. She turned to walk home and I heard a muffled sob. That moment I knew I loved her. I waited for her to turn the corner, then ran the long way to her house. I was waiting for her with open arms. Now comes a particularly embarrassing part. As she began to speak, I took my fingers to her lips and said, "Shhhhh, we don't talk about this. I am still angry, but I love you through my anger." I turned and went home. This time I *did* call in the morning.

After high school, love could be proved by *not* having sex—with other people. I accused one girlfriend of constantly wanting me to prove my love to her. She said it was easy: "All I want is that you don't sleep with any of the old lovers or would-be lovers who keep coming around."

A few years ago I thought about all this as I rode the train from New York City to Vassar College, where I was to lecture on educational reform. The invitation had come at a good time, for I was wallowing in the swamps of my dissertation research. Someone at Vassar had read my article "Paulo Freire: Report to the Principal's Office Immediately" and wanted to hear more. I was flattered and thrilled; just the invitation—which I taped on my wall along with the envelope it came in—led to a pickup in my productivity. I was being taken seriously by a college that was taken seriously. I told David, an old friend from high school, about the lecture, and he said, "This is what we always dreamed of: *lecturing at Vassar!* God, I remember in college going there to try to pick up girls. Now you're a lecturer. You'll have your pick."

I hadn't looked at it that way, but it sounded plausible. There would be dinner with students and faculty, and a reception after the lecture. Yes, there would be opportunities, and I wouldn't have to introduce myself. I might even be looked at as a prize of sorts.

This fantasy was muted by the fact that I was in the early stages of love with Sandra, who was long past being an undergraduate. We had motion in our relationship, occasional magic, and even a little mystery (but not so much as to make me crazy). The problem was she lived with another man. That relationship was essentially over, she talked about getting her own place, but they still used the same bed.

If I had been younger than I was when I met her, I would have been excited by the prospect of an *affair*, a *triangle*. If it happened now, in my early thirties, I would say to her: "Get yourself straightened out and then give me a call." But at twenty-seven, I took a deep breath and went cautiously into a relationship, resolving to give it up if it wasn't resolved within two months. In the meantime, I was free to see other women. In theory. Actually, I saw only Sandra and was content, even after three months.

After I told Sandra about the Vassar Lecture, she brought over a bottle of champagne to celebrate. But the night before I was to go, as I excitedly read her my notes, she became withdrawn.

"What's the matter?"

"All those girls. They'll be all over you."

"For one thing, Vassar is co-ed these days."

"Yeah, but you're lecturing about education. We haven't progressed *that* far—you'll get mostly girls. You'll be fiery, rouse their spirits, raise their hopes. They'd have so much to learn by sharing a few intimate moments with you."

"Sounds like you speak from experience."

"And you'll do it, too, if for no other reason than to get back at me for being slow about leaving Jim. Oh, you'll be so charming."

"I'll do my best to be dull," I said, trying to joke my way out of making any promises.

Sandra and David had assembled a tempting scenario. It would probably do Sandra good to learn that until she was there for me to come home to, there'd be no reason for me to come home. She was close to tears.

"Look, I don't even know if I'm going to spend the night. There's a late train back and we left it open."

"I'm sure you'll get an offer to stay. Or you'll just be 'too tired' to travel. Or the reception will go on and on and no one will realize the time and then some senior will rush you to the station but make sure you get there too late. And there you'll be, stranded in Poughkeepsie in the dead of winter, and she'll say, 'Why not, let's get an Irish coffee.' Or, that professor woman will ask you to stay over so you can visit her class in the morning because 'there's *so* much more we'd like to ask you.'" Sandra was smiling now, but I was enjoying myself more than she was.

Actually, I wasn't as excited about the sexual opportunities as I was about the aura of adulation Sandra predicted. I didn't want groupies as much as I wanted *education* groupies. I had been writing cranky articles in obscure journals for years, and now it looked like someone thought I was on to something. I hoped so.

"I'm happy for you, really. It's my fault we're in such a crazy position because I can't get it together to leave Jim. I want to share this with you as much as possible. I want to be there when you get home. Seriously, do what you want, but if you *do* make it home tomorrow night, you'll be high from your triumph and want to stay up talking. I'll be here to listen. Give me the extra set of keys, and I'll spend the evening here. If you come home at two a.m. it'll be wonderful."

"But what if I don't come home? I mean, it's possible I won't make that last train even with*out* a lustful student. This is important, and I have to be flexible. I can't feel pressure to make that train."

"Oh, that'll be okay, really. Then I'd see you after work the next day. If nothing else, at least I won't be spending the night with Jim. Look, if we wind up together I'm going to have to get used to the fact that there will be other college trips. It'll be good practice."

She was so accommodating, so desperate. I smiled and got the keys for her, then walked her to the subway.

As I rode up the Hudson, instead of thinking about the most important talk of my young career, I thought about Sandra alone late that night in my small apartment: listening to Billie Holiday's "Lover Man," hoping that hers was on a southbound train; regretting all that wasted time with Jim, time lost to us; being attacked by images of me acting insufferably with a Vassar student and getting away with it.

I decided to come home no matter what. Prove my love. A magical night. I'd tell her about the lecture, and we'd make quick, passionate love. Then longer. Night would stretch into morning and she would go to work unable to bear the thought of returning to dead Jim and their dead bed. Even though we had agreed that my apartment was too small for us, she would stay there until we could get someplace bigger.

My coming home would be the proof she needed in order to risk losing the security of Jim (dead men don't walk) in favor of me, who, she feared, was too unsettled, too involved with work, and who liked her because I didn't have to be responsible to her. I'd come home to show her that an affair wasn't all I wanted, or could handle.

I stepped off the train in Poughkeepsie, resolved that I'd be stepping back on late that night.

I was greeted by Margaret Campbell, the professor who had arranged the lecture. She was in her midthirties, younger than I had pictured her during our phone conversation, when she'd told me to look around the platform for "the lady with the blue dress."

"Here I am, 'the lady with the blue dress,' " she said cheerfully. "And there you are, 'the man with the brown book bag.' My students are really looking forward to this. We had a mock debate about your article last week, and I had a hell of a time getting someone to take the negative."

I was at the top of my game. My lecture was passionate and angry, with just enough wit and self-effacement to avoid getting into an adversary relationship with those who disagreed. There were several challenges during the question segment— whoever wound up arguing the "negative" must have done a good job. A couple of questions troubled but didn't overwhelm me, and I finished with an incentive to get deeper into my research. "Provocative, quite," Margaret said as she handed me a glass of wine at the reception.

An hour later, five students—all women—remained to continue the dialogue and finish the wine. All had done some work with children and were considering careers in education, so my experiences in Mexico, Bedford-Stuyvesant, and with VISTA were of more than academic interest to them. One had asked me at dinner about the possibility of doing a summer internship with me on my research grant, but now I couldn't remember which one.

I had been going on adrenaline, acting effectively but not really enjoying myself (I couldn't remember the taste of anything I'd eaten at dinner). Suddenly I relaxed and the room came into focus. I smiled at where I was, and with whom: it was exactly the way Sandra and David had predicted. I was surrounded by female admirers in the antique plushness of a reception room at Vassar College. Good, I thought, this gives me the opportunity to really prove my love. I could allow myself the pleasure of temptation, knowing it would only make my gesture more powerful.

Carol, a senior from Philadelphia, sat next to me on a blue velvet couch. Judith and Monica sat cross-legged on the thick gray carpet. Margaret talked animatedly to Deborah; twice I heard my name mentioned. It was all I could do to keep from laughing. Carol started telling me about her boyfriend, then corrected herself: "*Ex*-boyfriend. I don't know why I'm telling you all this, I think I'm a little drunk, except we had planned on opening a little school together. Did you ever think of doing that? Otherwise you'll always be fighting the goddamn system."

Monica started writing into a pocket notebook. "I just remembered I'm covering this for the paper. My roommate's an editor and when I said I was going to a lecture she said she'd trade me use of her car tomorrow for five hundred words. You don't mind if I make up quotes, do you, I forgot to take notes. Maybe we can talk later; or tomorrow, are you going to be around?"

I looked at my watch. A little past 10:30. The last train was in an hour. "No, in fact I should get going," I said, standing up. Time for me to pay the price of my love. I knew there was no such thing as a free lunch, but hadn't realized how steep the check would be. Margaret upped the cost by offering her house. "A nice country house, lots of rooms, beautiful wood, tons of books. Not much furniture yet, but plenty to read around the fire." She didn't mention if a husband was included in the picture. She wasn't wearing a ring, but I'd been fooled before.

The motion for me to stay was seconded by Judith. "That way you can come to class tomorrow."

"Yeah, that would be neat," Deborah said.

"And I can get my quotes straight," Monica added. Carol was silent. Was it because Margaret had made an offer before she could get around to it; how could she compete with her professor?

"Look, it's getting close to eleven. We'll never make that train," Margaret said, though my watch said 10:45.

"Sure you can, it's only fifteen minutes away and the damn train never shows up on time anyway," Carol said.

Did she really want me to leave: if she couldn't have me, then no one could? Or was I getting carried away to think that *any* of them wanted me? Well, even if I *was* getting carried away, I was enjoying the ride and didn't want to get off. I looked closely at Carol: pale green eyes, smooth skin, brown hair falling soft and straight. She went to take a sip of wine, but her glass was empty. She shuddered slightly—I realized how chilly it was—and pulled her unbuttoned sweater across her chest by crossing her heart with her arms. We were in Poughkeepsie in the middle of winter and I wanted to reach out and make her—us—warm. I had made no promise to Sandra, she knew nothing of this little test of my love. Damn it, she *lived* with someone. If I didn't come back, it would shake her up; whereas if I came home, she'd think she had me in her pocket, and why not continue to take her sweet time sorting out her options? And it could be good for my career if I stayed. Have lunch with the department chairman: "Why don't you send up your vitae." Carol leaned back and closed her eyes. The others were cleaning up. I sat back down. If I touched her cheek, ever so slightly, she would sigh so achingly that I could never leave her.

She opened her eyes and said, "I'd really like to talk to you more, sometime."

I stood up quickly and said to everyone, "Listen, I've got a pile on my desk I'd better get to first thing in the morning. You've all given me a lot to think about." I said nothing about Sandra, who in a couple of hours would be brushing her hair dry, straining to hear the zip of a key in the lock. The embrace. The love. The doubt no more, for either of us. Yes, this was what I wanted more than a dorm room with a stranger ("Shhhhh, you'll wake my roommate") or the guest room of a professor ("I'd like you to meet my husband, he had to stay home and finish his novel").

I said good-bye to Judith, Monica, Deborah, and Carol ("Maybe I'll write you sometime"), and Margaret drove me to the station, encouraged me to keep those articles coming, and left me to wait forty-five minutes in the cold for the tardy train.

The train wasn't much warmer. Someone blared bad rock music from the back of the car, and no one had the guts to ask him to turn it down. The Hudson River, which had matched the blue sky on the trip up, now blended with the blackness. A heavy woman was sitting across from me with a sleeping child on her lap. I was in the uncomfortable limbo of fighting sleep. I didn't want to sleep, afraid that I'd awaken bereft of the buoyant feeling that most was right with the world and the rest could be fixed. The bass and drums from the tape recorder embedded in my ears like cotton swabs, obscuring the rumbling of the train. My left foot tapped in consort with the enemy.

As we approached the lights of the Bronx, the music stopped and the heavy woman woke her child, who rubbed his eyes and embraced her neck. In the tunnel, the conductor reminded us to take our personal belongings. I remembered the first time I saw Sandra.

She was sitting alone in a jazz club, reading a book between sets. David pointed her out to me and said, "Now there's someone who's unapproachable." She was a few years older than I, my first lover with a future *and* a past; the first to cut her hair short and not lose her appeal to me; the first who understood my work without being part of it. I bolted out of the train as the others stretched and yawned.

I took the shuttle to Times Square and leaped into an uptown local as the doors were closing. I resented every stop the subway made, as if the conductor had no understanding of the purpose of this trip. Two teenagers looked stoned and scared to go home. Although the train was almost empty, a thin, elderly man in a brown suit stood, holding on to a strap while reading the *News*. I felt attached to the teenagers, the old man, the heavy woman, the child, even the one who had blared the music. I would never know what happened to any of them, and they wouldn't hear about my night with Sandra. It was good that the Poughkeepsie train had been late; her doubts would swell and I would burst them, feasting on the love that would pour out.

I slowly turned the key in the lock as if it were a task requiring delicacy and skill. The living room was dark; I panicked. I hadn't considered the possibility of her not being there. Jim must have picked that night to save their relationship, begging her to stay with him, he needed her. Light crept from under the bedroom door. I had turned off that light. Why wasn't she coming out to greet me? She must have fallen asleep clutching the pillow.

I went into the bedroom. Sandra was flat on her back on the bed with her clothes on. She struggled groggily to get up. Yes, I had wakened her. She stumbled back into a prone position, then turned on her side, propped her elbow on the pillow, and rested her head on the pedestal of her hand. It couldn't hold the weight. "Hi," she said, grinning but not with excitement or passion. Her eyes were awake but not alive. My emotions sank to my feet, which became too heavy for me to move toward her. She was drunk.

"Did you have a good time? Tell me all about it, everything."

"Are you drunk?"

"Well, yeah, I guess, but that's okay. I can't talk too well, but I can listen. Tell me. Did you have a good time?" Her words sounded rehearsed; once she gave my cue I would do all the work.

"Yes, it went great. Why are you drunk?"

"I don't know," she yawned. "It was a surprise. I went to Donnie and Sue's—you remember them, or maybe you never met them. Anyway, they live down the block. They went to school with Jim and me. Anyway, I hadn't eaten dinner, some guy came over with wine. I didn't realize I was getting drunk. I felt fine. But as soon as I got outside, oh boy. What time is it?"

"Two."

"Well, go *on,* tell me about it. A bedtime story. If I fall asleep, just remember where you left off, and tell me the rest in the morning."

My feelings were no longer lodged in my feet. They were all over, and they were furious. Now I could move, but I had nowhere to go. How could she have done this? Didn't she realize how stupid it was? Who was this guy with the wine anyway? She had wanted so much to be with me but made it impossible. Her fantasy about me at Vassar had come true, but not my fantasy for after Vassar, and it was due to her undoing. No magic. Only mystery, deep goings-on. I was losing my taste for mystery.

I went into the bathroom, hoping she would make a quick recovery and call in after me. When I emerged, she was under the cover, asleep. Her clothes lay undressed of her in a pile on the floor. I almost wept at her empty jeans, her shirt, her underwear.

I sat for a long time in the living room, lit only by the blue light of the soundless TV. Every few minutes I checked to see what was going on: A man was looking for something or someone that other men were trying to make it impossible for him to find. His car went off the road. He punched and got punched. He was released from jail (I hadn't seen him go in). All to the soundtrack of the bass and drums from the train.

Finally, I went to bed, careful not to wake Sandra. If I had been younger, I might have rented a car and magically showed up at Carol's dorm ("I'm so glad. I have a single room and no classes till noon"). If I had been older, I might have wakened Sandra and had angry sex with her, with thrusts like little-boy punches leading to welcome unconsciousness. But on that night sex wasn't something I drove two hours to get from a stranger. Nor was it something I wanted in anger.

Several times during the night Sandra reached out for me in her sleep, once groaning. Each time I moved away, till I fell asleep against the wall.

In the morning Sandra rushed to get dressed so she wouldn't be late for work. I was too sleepy to be angry so I stayed in bed.

"Boy, were you mad at me last night! A couple of times I woke up and you wouldn't have anything to do with me. I'm sorry, I just didn't realize I was getting that drunk."

"How *could* you?" I asked, although I knew that people don't do things like that and know why in the morning.

"How could I *what?* Get that drunk? I don't know, maybe because I've been so tired all week. Those late hours we keep." She rolled her eyes seductively and laughed as she threw her clothes from the night before into a canvas bag.

"That's probably it, because I don't even have a hangover. It was just exhaustion."

She gave me a quick kiss on the mouth, then bobbed her head back down for another, lingering kiss, which I opened my mouth for. Then she was gone, locking the door from the outside, which meant she had taken the keys.

I took inventory: I had done well at Vassar; my work was solid. In spite of being attracted to Carol, I had truly wanted to come home. It could have been worse; at least Sandra had been there. Isn't home the place you go to collapse?

I went to the library and did some research. Two ideas had circled around me the night before, just beyond my grasp. By 4:00 p.m. I could feel them clinging to my fingertips. I called Sandra at work and blurted, "You know, I came home last night to prove my love."

"How sweet," she replied, "but you don't have to prove anything to me. You've proved it with your passion and your patience. Listen, I've got to run, I'll see you tomorrow night. Sober. Promise. I love you."

The next night she was waiting for me when I came home. We made love for an hour before going out to dinner. Over coffee I told her she had two weeks to leave Jim. She started to cry.

The Green Grass of Flatbush

The mailing lists must have gotten mixed up. The only people who show up at the biggest party I have ever attempted to give are those who, over the years, have been deleted from the Christmas Card List. I shouldn't have trusted the kids to send out the invitations, but I wanted them to feel involved so they wouldn't resent the intrusion into their little routines.

Strange that they would mess up so badly. Billy gets such good grades and has been praised by his fifth-grade teacher, Ms. Corchoran, for his "creative thinking." Mr. Brenner calls third-grader Janey "a plugger," and at my office the pluggers are highly trusted. Billy and Janey are always at each other's throats, another reason for this team project.

Ah ha! They planned it. I can tell by the way they linger in the living room as the guests arrive, rather than scurry upstairs, downstairs, or out entirely.

The guests are polite, none mentioning the circumstances that led me to cast them aside. My former broker admires how much we've "done with the place." Doesn't he realize that this isn't "the place" he knows? *That* house was in Yonkers, not Bronxville, and was lost in the unexpected (by him) dip in the market that he laughingly referred to as the "Mud Slide of '81," which he was sorry I had to get caught under. Perhaps he doesn't want to notice how well I've done since.

My former analyst arrives, the one who phoned my mother late one night to scold her for her long-ago escapades with the head of the Ebbets Field grounds crew while my father was with the team on the road. Highly unprofessional, he agreed at my next—and last—session, but he was too angry at my mother's betrayal against his hero "to let it go without some closure."

He softly inquires as to the health of my folks. I reply, "I have given up all hope of coming to terms with them and have completely evicted them from my life," when there they are glued to the doorstep. A beaming Billy assures them that the welcome mat under their feet applies to them. They hobble in, waving their invitations like flags.

The guests are sprinting through the whiskey and bourbon; our usual guests concentrate on the Soave and pace themselves like marathon runners. Janey escorts in an oddly appealing woman in a flowered dress. My ex-wife. My memory-movie reels backward as she comes forward: the indifference, the bitterness, the rage, the questions, the jealousies, the doubts, the passion, the unfolding, the explorations, the first sighting—her approaching me shyly at a party. Her hair is short now, streaked with thin, gray rivers. She nudges her mouth into a questioning smile.

"How sweet of you to think of me, there were so many times I thought of inviting you to my place but couldn't bring myself to do it and now I am ashamed and touched that you were big enough to make the first move. And look at all these familiar faces. It's so nice that you've kept in touch with so many old friends."

"Yes," I reply, "I think it's very important to have enduring relationships," waving my hand around the room at the array of ex-friends, ex-lovers, ex-mailmen, ex-superintendents of long-demolished buildings. I notice two members of an ashram I sat silently in during a few uncertain weeks in my midtwenties. The former Congressman I once campaigned for is telling them about his bribery trial. They nod with great interest, lips sealed.

My current wife can't figure out what is happening, but she is too busy to ask, renewing acquaintances and replenishing the spread of cheese, crudités, and sour cream–cucumber dip. Billy giggles as he points to various guests while jabbing Janey in the ribs. She doesn't fully understand the humor but emits her sweet, innocent, joyful laugh at seeing Daddy squirm.

And now that laugh blesses my ears in stereo: high-pitched from my daughter, and deeper from my ex-wife standing next to her. With all the drinks I've had, I think for a moment that Janey is actually my daughter from a previous marriage, but no, her bone structure is unlike my ex-wife's, unlike mine—like my current wife's. Janey looks overwhelmed by all the emotion in the room.

My father creaks toward me: the man I worshipped as a child, failed miserably to emulate as a teen, tried to forgive as a young adult, and succeeded in forgetting as a mature man. He was the Golden Wing of the Brooklyn Dodgers, which made me the envy of the neighborhood kids. "Is he really your *father?*" new kids would ask when they saw a picture of the man with my name and bone structure in the *Daily News* or *Mirror.* Rarely did they see the actual man, at least not with me. They didn't have to deal with my father's road trips, which led to my mother's side trips.

Out on the field I could never get my fastball to zip or convince my curve to deceive. No one could understand that, least of all my father. For me, life was one long away game.

Look at him now: the golden arm dangles tremulously from the frail body that disguises my memory-image of him.

"Hey, sonny boy, remember this?" he says and goes into a pale imitation of his "patented" windup—looking like I did in my playing days—grunting with each stuttering movement. This is how he used to "playfully" punch me. He'd wind up and throw a stinging rap to my cheek, punctuated by his rasping laugh. "You're my sonny boy, yes you are," he'd say, both of us knowing that all I had received in the genetic relay race was his bone structure.

I start to bail out as his beanball fist balloons toward my skull. But he releases instead a looping change-up that curves into a big hug. "You're my sonny boy, yes you are. Let's take a swing up to Cooperstown soon. You know, they got a gold-plated cast of my arm there—that's the only part of me that made the Hall, but it's the most important part." Yes, I know they have a cast of his arm. I read about it in the papers.

So many times he promised to take me to Cooperstown when I was a kid. "This time I mean it," he says, reading my mind like parents do, like he never did. My mother joins us; the ghost of a beautiful young woman inhabits the sagging skin of her face. Her eyes implore, and I feel mine granting absolution.

The *Mirror* is gone, and the *News* is almost respectable. People cook, make love, and pace the floors where Ebbets Field used to be. The men who tended its grounds are dispersed among places like Miami and Phoenix, where they mow retirement lawns and dream of the green grass of Flatbush, the white ball scampering across their handiwork.

"I'm so glad you asked us," my mother says. "Maybe you and the family can join us for the Fourth of July. We never had a family Fourth when you were a boy, what with your father always working."

My wife goes out for more Jack Daniels and Wild Turkey. The kids, tired of their creation, go upstairs. I am left alone with my past. Where is this party leading? Ahead or back? I try to remember what Einstein meant by the space-time continuum. The galaxies are receding from one another. If I knew why, would that help me understand my mother's skin, my father's arm, my ex-wife's hair? None of these things are like they ever were. Time has passed but time is here. They are here.

"There's never enough time," my mother says.

"No, Mom, time is the only thing we have as much of as we can use. It is the only thing that is always with us."

"Such a philosopher, that's what I always used to say about you," she says.

"Yeah," my father chirps in, "I don't know where he got those brains, certainly not from me. I was scared to death of you, sonny boy."

"The-party's-over," my father sings, like they say he did in the locker room shower after each game, win or lose. "Little-boy-you've-had-a-busy-day," my mother coos as she tousles my hair, like she used to while I bathed, whether I had had a busy day or not. It would make me feel worthy of sleep. They leave, lighter afoot.

The only people left in the living room are my wife and ex-wife. They are making plans of some sort. I haven't really looked at my wife all night, or lately. Her eyelids encroach on the gray-blue irises. A good night's sleep will remove only a fraction of the weathering from her thin, angular face. Once, soon after we met, I kissed her when we got stuck in a pedestrian gridlock while exiting the subway at Grand Central Station. Her eyelids were half-closed then, too. She excuses herself to check on the kids, something she hasn't done recently.

"Thanks for the wonderful party," my ex-wife says. "Your wife is wonderful. I love the kids."

"Yes, the kids are great. My wife is great. Everything is great. Where did we go wrong?"

"Oh, I think it was just bad timing."

"Yes," I reply, "bad timing. We can't control time, but we should try to do something about timing."

"You've developed into quite the philosopher," she says with surprised admiration.

from
The Swan Song of Vaudeville: Tales and Takes

In the City of Mystery

In the city of mystery the road signs are changed hourly. You never know who will show up at your door with flowers. Or a knife.

The movie theater skips the first and last reels. The newspaper puts all the names on page one, and the stories minus names on the inside pages.

Each morning you find footprints in your yard; every afternoon there is fog; in the evening a wailing comes from just over the ridge.

The door to the judge's chambers says Crater, and the office at the airport says Earhart.

Lovers turn their backs on you, and when they come around you don't recognize them. Strangers leap into your arms at the supermarket.

You awaken each morning after a night of dull dreams eager to start the day.

Lonely

You walk the late-afternoon streets.

A cop enters a coffee shop to get something to go, leaving his partner outside. The partner paces, lonely, wondering what's taking so long.

The faint moon is lonely in the blue sky.

A woman in a pink dress walks a dog. The dog is lonely for other dogs and tugs whenever he sees one. The problem of this dog's loneliness cannot be solved by the company of the woman in pink.

The woman in pink is lonely. The companionship of the dog helps, but is not enough.

A beggar posted at a subway exit gets lonely between trains.

"In the Wee Small Hours of the Morning" wails from the window of a cheap hotel.

The sun sets, and in rooms where lights do not go on, lonely people sit in the dark.

The moon is covered by a single, lonely cloud; they will soon drift apart.

You weave among them all, eyes open, breathing, listening, keeping your composure, not letting them know that you know.

Somewhere a Phone Is Ringing

Somewhere a phone is ringing on a hot summer night. You don't make note of it until the tenth or twelfth ring. After the twentieth or so, you wonder how long the caller will let it ring.

Still ringing when you go to bed at 1:30 a.m., receding as you ease behind the scrim of sleep. Each time you wake, you determine that the rings have not entered your dreams but are present in the night.

You think:

Perhaps, a man is calling his ex-girlfriend. He brandishes the phone as she cowers in the corner of her studio apartment. If she lifts the receiver to yell "Hang up!" he will shout her name and be back in her life.

Maybe she's not home and his desperate ringing is for naught, but how can he be sure? If she is there and he hangs up he will have lost her forever.

Maybe he knows she's not home but she has a parrot that will drive her crazy with telephone ringing for the next forty years.

Maybe he's not home. He punched in her number and left his apartment. He's with another woman, getting off on the image of his old girlfriend cowering in the corner.

You choose a more felicitous scenario:

Lovers separated by the continent, entwined in the ringing of their love in each other's ears.

At 8:30 a.m. the phone is ringing as you eat breakfast. It is all right by you.

Woolworths Parakeets

Hundreds of Woolworths are closing, and thousands of generic parakeets will be released on noon of the final day. Scrawny blue-and-green ten-dollar birds will scatter in downtown Las Vegas, uptown New York City, and suburban Lynbrook. They will be freed from their group homes, where they sleep leaning on each other like passengers on a midnight train in India. These are not the cream of the exotic bird crop; they are bred for volume, their markup too low to help keep Woolworths in flight. If you see one in your neighborhood, coax it home with seeds and love. Let it fly freely around the house, offer it food off your plate, teach it the words you've longed for someone to say to you, and love it as you love the America that once you knew.

The Swan Song of Vaudeville

I would see her silhouette sometimes through the shaded window of her room over the marquee.

Heart fluttering, I would go in and perform. Vaudeville was getting old, but I was young. Three years with the man in the bear suit, till he retired. By then I had developed enough characters to go out on my own, on the road for months at a time. But always back to the theater under the marquee under her room.

On nights when her light was off and the shade up, I would peek from behind the curtain until the house lights went down, searching the audience for her.

One night, during my ventriloquism bit, as the dummy sang "Love's Old Sweet Song" while I swallowed fire, I thought I heard an orgasm from above.

I transfigured the spit-take into high art, hilarious to everyone in the house except me.

That night my performance vaulted the walls of time, and my closing number is often considered to be the swan song of Vaudeville.

Ghostly

I feel a tapping on my shoulder. I live alone. No one else
has keys. My heart races as if trying to flee to a safer body.
But I am startled for only an instant. I turn around and, sure
enough, it's merely that ghost. He always shows up when I
feel most alive, which for a long time meant infrequent visits.
Lately I've come to expect him at least once a week.

He never uses fancy theatrics to frighten me. No creak-
ing footsteps from the closet or lightning bolts piercing the
bedroom wall. No howls or shrieks, no low moans or clank-
ing chains. "I'm not too good on the audiovisuals," he once
explained after trying to project hand-shadow ghouls onto
the wall.

Sometimes he hides behind a chair and emits a feeble
"Boo!"—and then, "Don't be scared, it's only me." Once,
I discovered the word *demon* written in what I thought was
blood on the front door. It turned out to be a jelly smear
from one of the doughnuts he'd brought as a treat. He apolo-
gized and then scrubbed the door clean.

Tonight it's just a tap on the shoulder. He shrugs, as if
to apologize for startling me. We sit for a while, until I forget why I was so cheerful. He has a smoky presence, vaguely
shaped into limbs and facial features—nothing I could grab
hold of, though God knows I've been afraid even to try.

Three days later, I return home from work feeling chip-
per. He is lying on the couch and rises with a start when I
close the door. "Huh! . . . Oh, it's only you," he says.

He seems weary, even more translucent than usual. I make
some coffee, and we drink it quietly. He dunks his cruller and

lets it dissolve in the blackness. The smoke from his cigarette looks like ghost-children wandering in the air.

"Anything wrong?" I ask.

He stares at the cold coffee. "There's something about living I'm beginning to miss," he says at last. "I can't remember what it is, not for the life of me." For the first time I think I see a flicker of a smile. He shrugs, and his borders undulate, giving the impression of a full-bodied fidget.

"Please go on," I say softly.

A bolt of lightning zips across the window, and he looks admiringly at it. "I thoroughly appreciated deadness," he says. "Now I feel almost nostalgic for the days when people disliked me for who I was, not for what I represent."

I reach out to touch him, forgetting how scared I've been to do that. He pulls away, though a coolness in my palm makes me think I might have grazed him. "Sorry," I say. "Only trying to help. You're fading away, pal."

"A throbbing where my bones used to be," he murmurs.

"Maybe you're coming back to life."

"I don't believe in that crap," he whispers as he merges with the last puff from his cigarette. Soon that too is gone, and I am alone in the room, which vibrates as if reacting to a tremor from someplace below. Traffic, no doubt.

In Continuum

Now, while the time since your death is still counted in weeks, I'll be walking along and there, just beyond my eyes' ability to distinguish faces, I'll see someone who looks like you, and for a few milliseconds my brain will form your face.

At first it was a little unnerving, but I've come to look forward to and treasure those milliseconds, and I will mourn them when they are gone.

God's Will

It is literally true: God created the heavens and the Earth, the waters and the living creatures, in six days. He rested on the seventh.

God really liked that seventh day, and continued to rest on His laurels. He *meant* to improve Earth, but after that first week He mostly let the free will He had bestowed run its course.

He did some standard maintenance and a few adjustments here and there, which left a lot of time to think about the two concepts that even He never really understood:

What preceded His own existence; even if truly nothing existed before Him, what exactly *is* nothing?

And, He had trouble with *infinity*. He knew He ruled all He could see, but how could He know for sure if He really saw all?

The two questions were entwined: If some force had created God, then maybe it had also created a place He wasn't privy to.

These questions occupied millennia of meditation, to little avail. But it made God quite sympathetic to those who devoted their lives to pure thought, such as theologians, poets, and sportswriters.

God felt warmly toward people of all religions. Whenever anyone mentioned "God," He knew they were referring to Him, since He had done it all, though often under an alias. God thoroughly enjoyed religious services, constantly scanning synagogues, churches, and mosques. He monitored individual prayers and kept a to-do list in His prodigious mind.

But whenever He was about to get back to work, those two bugaboos— nothingness and infinity—would get the better of Him, and He would continue His R&R: rest and rumination.

His calendar remained a month of Sundays.

Regret gnawed at Him. Maybe if He had worked on that original seventh day, when He was on a roll, He might have created better methods than war and illness to provide constant changes in the cast of characters. (Though God had to admit that He was hooked on the drama; He was the supreme channel surfer.)

One day He really would need to get back to work; in the meantime, what could those who scorned Him do to Him? One of His favorite expressions that humans had used their free will to compose was: "So, they'll call me *pisher*," meaning roughly: *All they can do is call me a name*. Whenever anyone took God's name in vain, or railed against Him, He would think: "Go ahead, call me *pisher*," sometimes adding, "You *stoonard*."

Then one day that infinity thing came to bite God on His divine ass. Somewhere out there *was* another God, who had created another heaven and fruitful planet. Could this be God's sibling, or maybe a superior breed of God? Now those damned questions weren't theoretical.

God learned about this other God through His all-knowingness. How this knowledge came to Him, He didn't know. He just knew.

He also knew that the other God had not rested on the seventh day. This God kept on working. This God had found a way to keep suffering in the abstract. On His planet everyone was an artist: they wept, they laughed, and they appreciated suffering, only experiencing it on stage and screen, on the canvas and the page. On His planet, heaven was a verifiable fact, so death was approached mournfully but without terror.

The astronomers created by the other God had found out about Earth and the physical suffering on it. In their prayers they implored their God to save the Earth from the legacy of neglect. Their God responded by making this proposal to the lazy God: "Clean up your act, make peace with the people of the Earth, or face my wrath. Because I can do more than call you *pisher,* you *dumbkopf.*"

Earth's God was not sure who had the leverage. Maybe the activist God wasn't as tough as He was hardworking. But since obviously Earth God didn't understand *everything,* He would take no chances. So, He did some divine genetic engineering, creating brilliant doctors, scientists, philosophers, and teachers of the arts. He smote phony preachers and imbued those who remained with an unimpeachable aura of credibility. The quality of life improved exponentially.

It was hard, nonstop work, but He came to rather enjoy it.

One day He realized that at some point He had stopped being aware of the other God; He was off the hook. Life on Earth was far from idyllic, but it wasn't so baffling. He could rest again, albeit briefly and occasionally.

On His first day of rest in ages, God snapped to attention. It occurred to Him that if He was as all-powerful and all-knowing as He had always believed Himself to be, it was possible that He Himself had planted the awareness of a superior God into His all-knowingness as a means of self-motivation. Humans had used their free will to fill shelves of Barnes & Noble with such gimmicks.

But if He remained at rest, He would forever grapple with holy doubt, waiting for the other cosmic shoe to drop. To play it safe, God vowed eternal vigilance and assistance. And they all lived happily ever after.

For One of Your Smiles . . .

An infant crawls away from home and lies down next to a river. He sleeps through puberty. When he wakes up and looks at his body, he realizes his absence must have caused a lot of pain. Fortunately for him, he is an adolescent and doesn't much care.

He falls back to sleep and reawakens middle-aged. Now the thought of his loved ones' grief makes him dizzy and he passes out.

He comes to. He is old and needs to stretch, to walk, to wander—the same sensations that got him into this predicament.

Somehow he makes his way back home. His mother sits on the porch swing weeping. She is unspeakably old, yet she cries with joy when she sees him: "My baby, my baby, you have returned."

He kneels by her side, and as she runs her hand through his thin white hair, she says, "So many times I have wondered where you were, what you were doing. Tell me everything."

He joins her on the swing, cradles her in his arms, and begins to tell her his dreams.

Love Potions and Bitter Pills

One

In a crowd someone laughed. Thinking, incorrectly, it was he, a woman said, "What a sad laugh." He smiled and was about to defend himself when she said, "But there's sweetness in your smile, so there's hope for you."

They went off together and he tried not to laugh. A week later, when the joy was too much, he bellowed. She declared, correctly, "I have changed your life."

Two

"Ah, an imperfect beauty," he said as he noticed the scar that whispered along her upper lip.

Perhaps that horrible moment of shattered glass was worth it after all, she thought.

Then she thought again.

Three

The world seemed to have doubled its offering: his two eyes and two ears were no longer sufficient. Only with their four eyes focused together and four ears tuned to the same frequency could he fully see the beauty in art and the sky, and completely hear the music of symphonies and breezes.

Four

In the past, the best that others could do was to help him forget death, briefly. With her, he could be reminded of death and still love life.

Five

They laughed and frolicked and kissed and nuzzled and ravaged and napped and did it all over again. She said, "They should slap a caption on us: In happier days."

Six

The voice on the radio was hysterical. They turned it up until they couldn't make out the words, drowning out the phone and sirens.

They shut the windows and harmonized in a hymn. Her hands threw scary shadow figures from her past onto the wall. His fist shadows pummeled them.

Seven

He was an incurable optimist until he swallowed her medicine.

Eight

He believed that her orgasms were authentic, but he started to suspect that she was faking her understanding:

"Oh. Oh. Oh.

"Yes. Yes. Yes.

"You poor thing, you!"

Nine

When he told her he loved her, he was caught red-hearted returning to the scene of someone else's crime. She studied him up and down as if cramming for an examination.

Ten

She made him beside himself, and he hardly recognized the man standing next to him.

Each time they parted, he was like a rocking chair she had quickly got out of.

Eleven

He ran away from her in circles, and she ran circles around him.

He surrendered, and she shredded his white flag.

He went limp and bared his jugular, like a vanquished fox, and she snapped at him.

"Okay, I give up," he said. "You win. I will fight on."

Twelve

She broke his heart in two. Then she quartered it.

But each portion regenerated.

Now he could run for miles, make love, weep at a sad movie, and still have one cold heart for her.

In a dream of drowning, his life flashed before his eyes. She wasn't there.

Thirteen

On her way out of town for the summer, she dropped by with a bottle of wine. He drove with her and they checked into a motel.

Afterward, he said this was far enough, he'd take the bus back.

This time she was the one who pleaded. This time he was the one who erupted. Anger poured from places in him where he didn't even know he had spouts.

Fourteen

The dust had settled and been swept away. He knew that there was a bulge under a rug somewhere, but frankly he didn't care.

They laughed all evening, and then she closed up on him. He stared at the CD player: No disc.

"You know," he said, "you don't have to turn a mountain around to get to the other side."

"God," she replied, "I am so sick of you."

Fifteen

He presented his case with eloquence, even incandescence. He kept at it, on a roll, a tongue/brain parley to beat the band, he felt his saliva effervesce, something chemical was afoot, he was foaming with rhetorical hegemony.

"You're perfectly right," she said, "and perfectly mad," as she eased herself out the door.

Sixteen

He finally got himself to dial her number. "Hello?" she asked, and he hung up, realizing he had no answer.

Seventeen

A night on the town, they agreed, like the old days, might fix it.

They did the cab-dance, to the pool-hall of mirrors. He set up; she broke and ran the table, the balls homing into his pockets. He could barely move when it was finally his turn.

Eighteen

It didn't matter how far they had gone from town. The landscape inside them was the same.

Their first worthwhile moments had been pure lust. Later, nostalgia joined the lust. Now, they talked of old times but ceased making new ones.

Nineteen

She put her finger on his wrist but could find no pulse. They disagreed on the implications.

Twenty

She held on to him long enough to convince him that if he said the right words she wouldn't leave.

He told her, "It's you and me against the world, babe."

She replied, "You are the world to me."

Twenty-One

She grew smaller as she walked away. When she became small enough, he would pick her up, look her in her tiny eyes, and assure her that she was safe with him, he would fix everything. But he lost track of her; she had grown too small for him to help.

Twenty-Two

He watched everyone in the world enter the room, except her. Now, even if she did show up, it might be too crowded. And what was she doing out there all alone?

Twenty-Three

The sadness of the empty dish after the unsatisfying meal.
No longing for the food, but the hunger was sorely missed.

Twenty-Four

A new one came along quickly. This one inexperienced, even
naive. Oh, his thirst for her.

Twenty-Five

How quick the quenching!
    His buried treasure. He broke her with his shovel.

Twenty-Six

The door opened shyly, just a crack, then blossomed into her
smile. "Let me tell you," she started, but the sentence was
never finished.

Epilogue

When he put on a black robe, she called him "your honor"
and abided by his judgments.

    When he put on a white smock, she called him "doctor,"
undressed for him without resistance or shame, and let him
heal her.

    When he put on a clown suit, she laughed out loud at
whatever he did, no matter how painful or sad.

    When he put on a gorilla suit, she kept her distance, but
threw him food and giggled as he scampered for it.

    Now he took everything off. She looked bewildered till
he began to cry, and she held him, rocked him gently, singing
him to sleep.

Uncollected

Application File

May 3

Your application has been received but not yet acknowledged. This response should not be inferred as being anything other than what it says.

May 11

We are pleased to acknowledge your application. We will now set out to get a clear sense of who you are. This will take time, as we take nothing and no one lightly. We are nothing if not thorough and we are thorough, which makes us truly something.

June 19

We write with the good news (to us—it will come as no news to you) that we have confirmed you are who you say you are and have done what you say you did. Now we address the task of evaluating who you are and what you have done. This is what we get up for in the morning, and what we think about when we fall asleep at night.

August 12

Our silence should not be construed as neglect or negativity. We merely misjudged our vacation schedules (we were done in by unintended consequences of the summer house share) and had a run of ill health (see previous parentheses). We barely have the people power to write these letters. We could use someone like who we think you are.

September 5

We are in need of additional supporting materials. You should be assured that our request reflects our voracious appetite for reading about you. Now that we are again at full strength, we lack enough of you to go around, and several of us are feeling bereft. In the event there are no teachers or employers untapped by your extensive dossier, we suggest that you take a temporary position and enroll in an evening course.

September 9

Could you provide us with a list of ex-lovers? If so, please describe the physical high and low moments of each relationship, from both points of view. Kindly indicate the circumstances in which each relationship was terminated and who, in your judgment, was at fault. Forgive the personal nature of this request. We are doing our part to ameliorate the blanket of anomie that pervades the workplace.

September 14

What is the origin of your last name? Has it been shortened? Your answer will be used for statistical purposes only.

September 17

Thank you for your interest in our company. Unfortunately, we do not have any appropriate openings at the present time. We shall endeavor to contact you should that situation change.

September 23

Please disregard the previous letter, which was the result of a clerical error. We regret any inconvenience. We might add that we found your response quite understandable.

October 9

We are pleased to offer you a personal interview. Due to renovations under way in our offices, we invite you to meet us at Chez Avec Amis, a cozy bistro in a quiet corner of town, tomorrow at 6:00 p.m. We have reserved the back room. Directions enclosed. Kindly bring any available photographs from the attached list. We apologize for the short notice, and assure you it is not the result of a last-minute cancellation.

October 11

Did you inadvertently happen to wind up with an extra left glove (tagged *vera pelle*)?

October 26

We have finally received completed reports from all those who attended your interview. (It is a good sign that we could barely pry people away from their computers.) We will now disperse into the field.

November 9

We have completed a series of meetings with your references. Not unexpectedly in matters of this kind, several issues have arisen. Kindly respond to the enclosed questions. Please understand—as we do—that the quoted material is no more—or less—than one version of the truth. (Two questions were inserted by one of us over the strenuous objections of many.)

November 15

We are pleased to tell you that we found your responses quite satisfactory; any new questions raised by your answers, we all agree, are better left untethered. And we are delighted to report that a suitable position has just opened up (please refer to parentheses in previous letter). As you can imagine, there is much paperwork to be done. You shall hear from us before the end of the year.

December 19

It is to our great chagrin that we will not be able to offer you a position, as our operations will be shut down immediately following completion of our open correspondence. There is widespread disagreement as to whether this cessation was precipitated by an inadequacy in our business plan or poor execution thereof. Suffice it to say, we all agree that had you begun this process sooner, the outcome would have been more felicitous.

January 2

It was kind of you to surprise us at Chez Avec Amis (you remembered!), and to pick up the check. Bringing the glove was a lovely touch. We are intrigued by your offer, and we feel we have much to contribute. The requisite paperwork is enclosed. We look forward to hearing from you at your earliest convenience.

To the Dying

Too much is asked of you, who must endure missions for closure from loved ones and enemies alike, while composing famous last words.

Overworked is no way to go.

Pretend you don't know those who crave absolution by robbing your last possession, time. Let them lay their burdens elsewhere instead of burying you in hastily quilted confessions. Surround yourself in your final harbor with those who truly appreciate the view.

As for those last words, that ship will sail on its own wind.

Excerpts from "Pausing and Looking Back" (1977)

I didn't plan to be a teacher of creative writing any more than I planned to be a creative writer. I arrived at each from a chance opportunity that acted as a catalyst for desire, determination, and talent.

I wasn't the kind of child who had a treasure chest of special books; I didn't sneak into a corner after dinner and write poetry or my autobiography. Until after college, most of my writing was for newspapers. My first fling with journalism came in fifth grade because I couldn't sing—or so the music teacher determined. He selected all but five of the kids in my class to be in the chorus. My teacher, perhaps in order to soften the blow, made us the newspaper staff. I carried on newspaper writing throughout high school and college. My attempts at creative writing were confined mostly to song lyrics. During the spring of my senior year (1970) I began writing fragmentary poems (influenced by Richard Brautigan) during brief respites from the campus protests I was involved with. Two days after graduation, I embarked on a career as a newspaper reporter.

My newspaper career lasted only a few months. (In a scene reminiscent of a grade-B newspaper movie, a senior editor advised me to "be a writer" while I was young and could deal with insecurities and frustrations.) I moved back to New York City, thinking I would write in-depth, novelistic, investigative, sensitive journalism. A friend told me of an ad in the *Village Voice* for a poetry workshop conducted by David Ignatow at the Ninety-Second Street Y. You had to send in six poems; twelve people would be selected. I had harbored secret poet fantasies, and I thought that the workshop could also help my prose writing, so I sent in six of the little poems I had written. I was accepted into the workshop, and my life changed. Journalism stepped into the backseat, and poetry got behind the wheel.

This is oversimplified, but I tell it because it is crucial to the attitude I bring to my students. I consider myself living proof that poets are not a separate breed of people recognizable at an early age. For many of us, an encouraging and sympathetic teacher can be of enormous help in our poetic growth. For me, it was David Ignatow in 1971. But who knows? If my fifth-grade teacher had decided that those not selected to be in the chorus would be the poets instead—and there was a group like Teachers & Writers Collaborative in those days to send someone to work with us—I might have begun my poetry career a lot earlier. So, when I go into a classroom, it is with the belief that any kid, despite previous signals, might connect with poetry, and that every kid is capable of creative expression.

My beginning as a teacher was also partly a matter of circumstance. I had heard of people who taught poetry writing to children, but I had never worked with young kids in any capacity and thought that I would need special training to attempt it. One afternoon during the fall of 1973, Stuart Milstein (a graduate school classmate) called and asked me if I could, on short notice, do a few poetry workshops in a Brooklyn elementary school, filling in for someone who had just dropped out of the program Stuart had organized. I was scared, but I said I'd try it. Stuart told me that Teachers & Writers Collaborative had some publications that might be of help.

There wasn't time for me to send away for the books, so I went to the T&W office, which was then a donated room in PS 3 in Greenwich Village. Entering the building, I realized I hadn't been in an elementary school for sixteen years. The sounds and smells seemed eerily similar to my old school so many years and miles away, and immediately I felt younger and smaller. Going up stairways and through halls gave me the déjà vu feeling of doing something wrong—a sensation that rose from sense-memories of going up the down stairs or being in the hallway when I wasn't supposed to. I knew T&W's office was on the fifth floor, but I didn't know which room. I poked my head into several classrooms before I found someone who pointed me in the right direction. By the time I found the room, I was exhausted and having second thoughts about making a reappearance in an elementary school disguised as a teacher. The kids wouldn't believe it for a second.

The Collaborative office was a classroom with stacks of books, envelopes, and papers. I walked in and shyly introduced myself to a man who was composing a letter. It was Steve Schrader, the director. I told him about the program I was going to be working in and asked him exactly what was Teachers & Writers Collaborative. He set aside his letter, gave me coffee, and talked to me about their work in the schools. I left the office with a pile of free books and an embryonic feeling of my future.

My sessions in Brooklyn were difficult but incredible, leaving me hungry for more. I participated in a T&W–supported training program led by Bill Zavatsky, and hooked up with my former elementary school for a series of workshops. I learned as I went along in the best place there is to learn: in front of a class. I submitted an article to the *Teachers & Writers Newsletter*. It was rejected, but Steve Schrader asked me if I would be interested in working in a school in Brooklyn the following fall.

So, when I meet someone who wants to do this kind of teaching but feels like an extensive background is needed, I respond the same way I do when someone says, "I'm not a poet," which is: "See what other people are doing; try it yourself."

Things happened quickly for me, with gigs from Teachers & Writers and Poets in the Schools, and an adjunct appointment in the City University. I had been making a living as an editor of an environmental magazine. Now I was a full-time teacher.

When I made my first appearances into classrooms, I always knew what I was going to do with the class. My creative pride, bordering on stubbornness, was such that I rarely went in with an exercise lifted directly from a book or another poet, at least not without twists or variations. Whenever possible, I tried to do things I had conceived from scratch; I might later find out something I thought I had invented had been done before, much to my annoyance.

Gradually, my presentations became more complicated, with more possibilities for individualized writing. I had an obsession to type immediately every good piece written by my students, so the work wouldn't vanish like unrecorded jazz improvisations. Many of these pieces became part of a canon of student work, serving as examples when I used the assignments with other classes.

As soon as I had developed a full bag of "teaching tricks," I realized that I often didn't use it, that teaching creativity means teaching creatively. It has less to do with formulas and more to do with human beings and familiarity with such processes as discovery, recall, adaptation, influence, connection, manipulation: the use of language to create, re-create, and, not to be forgotten, recreate.

Unlike Poets in the Schools, T&W focused on long-term residencies, so those sessions were like laboratories for me, where I was able to explore and experiment. For example, I had a group that was doing acceptable work, but their writing didn't compare to the excitement I heard in their voices in the hallways and out on the streets. One week I brought in a tape recorder and started doing dramatic improvisations with them. The kids opened up tremendously, and the results were reflected in their subsequent writing, long after the tape recorder was put away.

I've long since stopped looking for a sense of completion after a short-term residency. One does not have the time to explore in depth the possibilities of language, or of human relationships. Indeed, the feeling of incompletion indicates something wonderful has begun. I meet a lot of people, and we separate while our relationships are still brewing. I have had good-byes that are both sad experiences and affirmations that the children have discovered something they value during my time with them. I always hope we can see each other again. If not, I hope there is something that endures in memory.

It's the last day of a six-day residency. I have already said good-bye to two of my three classes. Something was missing in the good-byes—the pain of separation. The children seemed preoccupied; perhaps they were being defensive, not dealing with the fact that they probably will never see me again. Or perhaps I just haven't been all that important to them.

I have felt sluggish all day. The kids have an inability to spell coupled with an obsession with correct spelling, a combination that resulted in me spending too much of my time buzzing around the room, a high-paid spelling bee, instead of discussing matters of the soul with them. I tried to explain that I didn't care so much about spelling. Maybe they inferred that I didn't care so much about them.

As I approach the last class, I will myself to make this a strong one. I prefer parting that is sweet sorrow—I'd rather be wrenched from a good-bye embrace by an impatient bus driver than be pecked on the cheek by someone who turns away with a forced smile several minutes before the bus warms up.

I turn off the classroom lights and ask the kids to visualize the model poem as I read it to them. In the dusk, the children slide into a calmness rare for a fourth-grade class. I talk to them about the poem, about poetry in general, and then about me. The inertia of the day is shifting. I tell them how much I've liked being with them.

At the end of a successful writing session, I ask if there are any questions.

"This is the last day. You're not coming back," a girl says.

"That's not a question."

"Why aren't you coming back?"

"Because if I did, I'd be disappointing the kids at the school where I'm supposed to go next."

"What school? We'll transfer," someone else says.

"You can't, it's too far away."

"Then we'll go and beat them up and take you back here."

"You can't beat them up, it's a high school."

"We'll get our parents to beat them up."

Every call for questions about poetry is answered with a variation on why do I have to leave and when will I come back.

"Maybe next year," is the only truthful answer I can give.

Shortly before three o'clock, as they are putting on their coats, someone writes "I love you Alan" on the board. A girl whose name I never learned grabs my briefcase and runs around the room, yelling, "He can't leave without this."

I sit down on the desk with my feet on a chair and say, "I'll stay."

They cheer.

"But it's time for you to go, children, the buses are almost ready," the teacher says, injecting a dose of reality.

The girl with my briefcase says she'll make me a trade. "I'll give up the briefcase and keep you."

"How about if I take you with me?" I suggest.

They decide that the whole class will come with me.

We have now played out this good-bye for as long as possible. We go outside, and the kids board the buses. One by one, the buses pull away. I am left alone on the doorstep, waiting for my taxi.

Almost all the students at this school are black. Before I started a long-term residency there, I anticipated problems with the kids accepting me. (I also thought there would be some cultural adaptations I'd have to make, having gone to all-white schools until college.) I expected that sooner or later there would be some kind of racial confrontation, but after several months it still hadn't happened, and I began to forget about it. Until one afternoon, when I heard Thomas yell, "You stupid honky." I felt a combination of relief and apprehension; relief that the tension was broken, but apprehension that this was now going to be a problem. At least my preparedness wouldn't go to waste—I was about to have an interesting racial confrontation.

I asked Thomas to accompany me into the hall. He was scowling.

"Thomas, how long have we known each other?"

"About six months, I guess."

"Well, now, did you just discover that we are different colors?"

"What are you talking about, man?"

"Didn't you just call me a honky?"

Thomas looked at me quizzically, then replied, "I didn't call *you* a honky, I was talking to Shawn." Shawn is lighter skinned than the rest. "I wouldn't call you a honky."

I felt silly, embarrassed. "Oh," was all I could reply, "why not?"

Thomas seemed stumped by the obviousness of my question, and finally sputtered out: "Because you *are* one!"

A couple of weeks later, I heard someone else call Shawn a honky, the way kids might call someone fatso or four-eyes. I yelled out, "Hey, there's only one honky in this class, and I'm it." They laughed, very tolerantly.

As a writer I must fight distractions. It is sometimes a losing fight. But nobody tells me when to write; if it doesn't happen early in the morning, it might happen late at night. Writing under deadline is a different situation, of course, but there are rarely deadlines for poems or stories. You set your own pace, and sometimes even make poems out of your distractions. As a teacher, I ask kids to write at a preappointed time. And they must do it in a room with as many as thirty other kids. And so many distractions.

How can I compete with the first snowflakes of the year, as they delicately salvage an otherwise gloomy, rainy, late-November afternoon? First one kid spots them and is at the window, followed infectiously by half a dozen more. I've never seen this class so genuinely excited.

"Sit down, this is time for poetry," the teacher yells, meaning well. She is trying to help, saying, "Come on children, you've all seen snow before."

But we haven't seen snow for eight months, and there was hardly any snow the winter before. This is the only "first snow" we'll have this year, and it will probably last only a few minutes before it turns back into rain. My heart is with the kids who are scrambling for position at the window. I want to go outside with them.

Yes, discipline is an important factor in writing, or any other art. But so is spontaneity, so is joy. The children are not "misbehaving"; they are truly curious and in a state of wonder looking at that snow. *Curiosity* and *wonder:* exactly what I've been trying to get them to associate with writing.

We talk about the snow, and this leads us to "first times" and "reunions." They settle down to write, only occasionally glancing out the windows.

from
*The Writing Workshop
Note Book*

Not Knowing

The act of creation is often a quest rather than a re-quest. In his final interview, Kenneth Patchen talks about "a quality of searching, of clumsiness in the craft almost like Van Gogh, for example, whose breaking with tradition seems almost as though he didn't know what to do next. And I think this is the stance of the creator."

I crossed paths with the poet Gerald Stern, who spent a couple of days at the Interlochen Arts Academy when I was writer in residence. Over lunch, I gave him a book of my poetry, and at dinner he had some nice things to say about it. He especially liked a poem called "Swan," which I had added to the manuscript out of fondness, though I wasn't sure it would hold up to critical scrutiny. I asked Stern why he liked the poem—hoping he would articulate some literary quality to support my fondness for it—and he replied, "Because I got the feeling you didn't know what the hell you were doing." I did feel affirmed, and this attitude has helped me spawn many subsequent pieces. I treasure the luscious feeling I get when I don't know what the hell I am doing but I really want to keep doing it.

During a hospital stay after a head injury, Jorge Luis Borges was afraid to write poetry—which had been his primary form—because failure could confirm that he had not fully recovered his "mental integrity." He decided to minimize the risk by writing short stories. Borges later said, "If it hadn't been for that particular knock on the head I got, perhaps I would never have written short stories." He didn't know what the hell he was doing. But look what he did.

Poetic Delirium

Good writings happen to those who wait. Children's author Enid Blyton wrote to Peter McKellar—who was doing research for *Imagination and Thinking*—that she has "merely to open the sluice gates." With her portable typewriter on her knee, she waits with a blank mind: "The story is enacted in my mind's eye almost as if I had a private cinema screen there . . . I am in the happy position of being able to write a story and read it for the first time . . . Sometimes a character makes a joke . . . and I think, 'Well, I couldn't have thought of that myself in a hundred years!' And then I think, 'Well, who *did* think of it then?'"

The answer, of course, is: *she* did.

Sometimes you don't even need to wait at your keyboard. Rather than putting nose to the grindstone, you merely need the fortitude to put nose to the pillow: Mayakovsky tried for two days to come up with an image "to describe the tenderness a lonely man feels for his only love." He went to bed on the third night with a headache. During the night he "leapt out of bed half-awake" with the image of how much a crippled soldier "cherishes his one leg." In the dim light of a match, he wrote on a cigarette packet: "his one leg." When morning came, Mayakovsky puzzled for two hours over the phrase, wondering "how it had got there."

The answer, again, is: *he* put it there.

Unconscious material can rise to the top even when you are not waiting or sleeping, like an evasive song lyric or the dog's name in the *Thin Man* movies (I'll spare you: It was Asta). Mental knots often loosen spontaneously when you step away from the task. I was grappling with the title of a story, and the best I could come up with was "God's Work," which was close but no cigar—it didn't illuminate the entry-way into the story. I closed the file on my computer, and, while checking the five-day weather forecast for a place I was to visit in six days, it came to me: "God's Will." Cigar.

Writers spend countless hours looking for the precise word, the transcendent image, the felicitous turn of narrative. And doesn't it feel good when these things just come to us? The rub is that the chance of a spontaneous solution (while asleep or awake) can be in direct proportion to the amount of conscious work we have been doing. In getting your writing to soar, there is no such thing as a free launch.

The surrealists' notion that art and literature stem directly from the unconscious is quite appealing: just remove the lid of conscious effort and let your "automatic" pilot take over. For me, Vicente Huidobro was closer to the mark when he wrote about reason's role in organizing *poetic delirium:* "If reason and imagination do not work in unison, one or both will suffocate."

Baudelaire writes about "genius" as being childhood recaptured with "the analytical mind that enables it to bring order into the sum of experience, involuntarily amassed." And Max Jacob states it eloquently: "Lyricism belongs to the unconscious, but an unconscious under supervision."

With the unconscious doing so much of the work, the least we can do is supervise.

The admixture of hard work (laboring over one's writing) and dream work (reveling in poetic delirium) may sound contradictory, as does much advice you hear about writing. It serves well to embrace these contradictions in the spirit of F. Scott Fitzgerald's dictum: "The test of a first-rate intelligence is the ability to hold two opposed ideas in the mind at the same time, and still retain the ability to function." (A note of caution: Fitzgerald wrote this in an essay titled "The Crack-Up.")

Keeping Going—A Note on Process

One way to keep the work flowing is to be acquainted with the writing process. Researchers have confirmed what writers have always known: most writing is done in stages, and the stages are often repeated, not necessarily in order. Here is one model for this recursive process.

Prewrite: Notate, vegetate, cogitate.

Exploratory draft: Ragged and reckless, no stopping for red lights.

Developmental draft: Shaping and amplifying.

Revision for you: Am I saying what I want to say?

Revision for others: Will the reader know what I am saying?

Tidying up: Punctuation, grammar, spelling.

Writers constantly ease or jolt from one mode to another. You are revising one idea when another comes to mind, necessitating a shift to exploratory drafting. Or, you write early drafts with abandon and revise with tranquility, but after tidying up you return to gut instinct to undo or redo passages.

Be careful not to turn process into procedure. Use the writing process as a backbone but maintain a free spirit. You can polish the life out of that rare, brilliant early draft (lucky you). And, even though it is not protocol to worry about spelling and the like until the end of the process, sometimes I just can't continue with a first draft until I check a fact or look up a definition. (Perhaps I need a break to allow my unconscious to loosen a knot.)

The computer is a wonderful tool for writers, but it can blur the way we experience the process. Force yourself to rekey a piece from scratch at least once. You will likely find yourself making changes through your hands that you might not have conceived with just your eyes on the text.

Drafts produced with a computer tend not to be as discrete as they are with a typewriter or pen. By constantly deleting, cutting, and pasting on the screen, you may wind up with a final draft without any record of an entire previous version. Save each piece occasionally under different names so that you can consult earlier drafts.

As you revise, don't refer only to the most recent draft, sentencing all previous excisions and alterations to oblivion. Something may look better now than it did when you changed it. Or perhaps something that didn't work before, now succeeds in light of subsequent revisions. Before doing a final draft, have an *appeals session*, reviewing earlier decisions.

With all the emphasis on process and revision, what about Jack Kerouac's "spontaneous prose" ("Never afterthink to 'improve' or defray impressions") and "First thought, best thought," the notion that Allen Ginsberg adopted from his teacher Chögyam Trungpa? Such spontaneity didn't work for Flaubert, whose first thoughts left him with "monstrous negligences," which he overlaid with revision after revision. Can our "first-rate intelligence" cope with these seemingly opposed approaches?

Sure. Not everyone needs to work the same way. If spontaneous composition with little revision works for you, fine, but you're probably in the minority. Even Ginsberg emphasized that access to the spontaneous mind requires intense mental training, and he cautioned students that "first thought" doesn't mean "first cheap remark" or "talk-babble to the self." And, as Douglas Brinkley points out, Kerouac's legendary three-week binge typing *On the Road* on a continuous scroll was "the outcome of a fastidious process of outlining, chapter drafting, and trimming."

Even first thoughts that *are* the best usually need to be revised as you translate from thought to written language. Playfully, I can even imagine Trungpa's *first* thought being, "The first idea—no, image; no, thought—that occurs to you may be the very best you can ever come up with," before he sculpted it into "First thought, best thought."

Earlier, William Blake similarly said, "First thoughts are best in art, second thoughts in other matters," yet at the Metropolitan Museum of Art, I stared, spellbound, at a handwritten manuscript on which Blake had replaced *form* with *frame* in "The Tyger." I guess he thought, "On second thought: *frame.*"

To make it even more interesting: The expectation that you will revise with care may provide you with the cover you need to write without inhibition on a first draft, allowing you to get at those first thoughts that *are* indeed best. Charles Darwin noted: "Formerly I used to think about my sentences before writing them down; but for several years I have found that it saves time to scribble in a vile hand whole pages as quickly as I possibly can, contracting half the words; and then correct deliberately. Sentences thus scribbled down are often better ones than I could have written deliberately."

A new dictum: *Vile hand, best hand.*

The Doubting Companion

Do you sometimes get an inkling to write, only to stop yourself by thinking, *Nah, it won't be any good?*

I have no advice on how to answer the question, "Will it be good?" The bad news is that there is no way to know.

The good news is: the very question is no good.

Kurt Vonnegut used to start off our graduate school workshop by asking us what problems we were having with our writing, other than not having the time. The number one response was some version of self-doubt. Approach your writing with respectful fearlessness. Adopt Miles Davis's attitude: "I never think about not being able to do anything. I just pick up my horn and play the hell out of it."

If you follow only one piece of advice in this book, let it be: Don't ask yourself for permission to write based on the promise that something good will emerge. Don't take "Nah" for an answer. Just write the hell out of it.

Doubt and temporary failure are the artist's companions; they should be recognized, listened to, and overruled. For most, doubt never departs, and failure rarely stays away for long. Embrace them as allies. Doubt does not preclude success; consider this comment by John Steinbeck: "Although sometimes I have felt that I held fire in my hands and spread a page with shining—I have never lost the weight of clumsiness, of ignorance, of aching inability."

Join Steinbeck and these doubters:

Walker Percy wrote to Shelby Foote: "I've been in a long spell of accidie, anomie, and aridity in which, unlike the saints who writhe under the assaults of devils, I simply get sleepy and doze off." (Of course, no one truly in a state of accidie, anomie, and aridity could write this.)

"Beset with technical difficulties and doubts," Nabokov was carrying the first chapters of *Lolita* to the garden incinerator. Fortunately, his wife, Vera, stopped him. (I imagine her cajoling, "Vladimir! Don't take out the garbage!")

The great actor Charles Laughton was plagued by self-doubt, especially during the 1937 filming of *I, Claudius*, which was never completed. Laughton would put his head in costar Merle Oberon's lap and weep, "I can't find my character. I can't find the man." Years later, one of the cast members lamented that Laughton "needed sun and got frost" from the director. Laughton shows enough flashes of brilliance in the surviving footage to make the case that much was lost because no one did for *I, Claudius* what Vera Nabokov would do for *Lolita*.

I witnessed a conversation in the late 1960s between Allen Ginsberg and the painter Arnold Bittleman. Bittleman was describing how he would often paint deep into the night, look admiringly at his work, and go to bed convinced that he had created a great work of art—only to wake up and discover that someone must have broken in and ruined his painting. Ginsberg replied that he used to feel that way, but now, even as he is writing, he'll think: "This is the same old bleeeecchhh."

John Berryman didn't read reviews until he was thirty-five because "I had no skin on . . . I was afraid of being killed by some remark."

Francis Williams—who played trumpet with Duke Ellington—started out as a pianist in his hometown, Toledo.

Williams thought he was pretty good until he met a local piano player who was so much better that Williams decided to change instruments: how could he succeed in the piano world if he wasn't even the best in the neighborhood? Perhaps Williams made the right decision, but it was for the wrong reason: his neighbor in Toledo happened to be Art Tatum.

Notebooks

In October 1837, Ralph Waldo Emerson made a felicitous suggestion to a young neighbor, who recounted it in his new notebook: "'What are you doing now?' he asked, 'Do you keep a journal?' So I make my first entry to-day."

Good thing for Henry David Thoreau—and us—that Emerson asked. I don't know whether Thoreau had heard this suggestion before, but *you* surely have, and you'll hear it again now. Maintain a notebook; indeed, several notebooks of various shapes and sizes (one for the back pocket, one for the book bag, one for the desk, one as a computer file), including at least one special notebook (or a notebook bought in a special place).

You can transform a run-of-the-paper-mill notebook into something special. Jack Kerouac illustrated some of the covers of his spiral pocket notebooks (which he constantly mined for his novels). After seeing photographs of them, I painted some of my notebook covers (a terrific gestation activity).

Notebook writing should be unbound from the chains of perfection quest. Virginia Woolf described her diary writing as "rough & random." Keep your notebooks stocked with dreams, ideas for characters, odd thoughts (someday you may invent odd characters to think them), overheard dialogue, observations, and memories.

Write "nibble notes" (consisting of key words, idea kernels) during the day, instead of counting on a nighttime writing repast that may not happen (too tired, too much in love, or too overwhelmed with how much there is to write).

David Ignatow did not do this on the day he wrote in his journal, "This morning I had an insight into love and self-centeredness, as I walked the street on an errand, and now I can't recall it, pressed by duties at home."

Periodically "save" mental notes into your notebook before your mind's RAM fills up. Flesh out these notes before you forget what they mean. If you do forget, no problem. Mysterious entries detached from context may be transfigured into something more compelling than the original association.

Don't just write about current events. Try to direct your thinking into the past (or future), looking for "spots of time"—as Wordsworth calls them—with "distinct pre-eminence."

Aide-mémoire is a term used in diplomacy for "a written summary or outline of important items of a proposed agreement or diplomatic communication." It also means—less exotically—"an aid to the memory." Think: *Someday I want to write about this, but I don't have the time, energy, and/or perspective now, so I will get down as much as I can in the form of snippets, details, and notes to myself. I can tell instead of show with impunity.*

Sometimes, one can nail it with the aide-mémoire. Carolyn Forché's widely anthologized prose poem "The Colonel" started out as a memory that she pared down and rendered "whole, unlined and as precise as recollection would have it." The text got mixed in with a poetry manuscript. When someone read the manuscript and told Forché, "This is the best one. This is the best poem," she replied, "Oh, no. That's a mistake. That's not a poem." She found out that it was.

Notebook writing helps allay the fear that the last thing you wrote will be the last thing you will ever write (which is true only once, but let's not go there). The Earth's resources are divided between the renewable (fresh water, timber) and nonrenewable (fossil fuels, metals). Some writers fear their creativity is nonrenewable and they may run out of material. But as you create, seeds get dropped along the way for later cultivation. When you are in a productive groove, your brain often comes up with more than you can handle; keep those seeds in your notebooks for arid days.

The notebook's value goes beyond being a repository of material. The very act of memorializing observations, events, and imaginings contributes to the skills integral to one's identity and growth as a writer, just as taking numerous photographs will improve your photographic ability and enable you to see more and see deeper. Virginia Woolf wrote in her diary—about her diary writing—that she could "trace some increase of ease in my professional writing which I attribute to my casual half hours after tea." (Ah, those half hours after tea!)

Noble Failures

We have all wished we could go back in time and make something better, given what we know now. You can do this with pieces of writing, but only if you keep track of them. Maintain a folder of deserving pieces that never quite made it. (Sometimes, you don't even have to do much to make a "failed" piece work—it was working all along, and you hadn't realized it.) Robert Lowell dived back into "three incoherent sketches" and "cut, added, and tinkered"; he emerged with "For the Union Dead."

One of my most satisfying writing experiences was beside a pool on a spring day in northern Michigan. My friend insisted on going swimming at the Holiday Inn, and I insisted on not going. We compromised: I'd go but not swim. I grabbed my failure-folder and pulled up a chaise next to the deep end.

I came across a short story that an editor had deemed "too slight rather than too short," adding the cutting trope, "if you catch the difference." Yes, I caught the difference; I just didn't know what to do about it. But there, by the pool, something happened. I filled the margins and interlinear space with notes, words, and arrows. I lost track of time. My friend stopped swimming. I kept writing. The story won an award. Perhaps my friend has a lovely memory of swimming.

What Do You Need to Know and When?

How much do you need to know before you start writing?

Sometimes you just need an impetus, which can be as amorphous as a sensation, a flash of memory, a dream, a phrase. Like a detective, you follow the impetus to see what secrets it might reveal. Jorge Amado told the *New York Times Book Review*, "I'm incapable of imagining a story from beginning to end. I never know what's going to happen next. I just follow where the characters lead me."

It helps to have a strongly felt sense of form, honed through years of reading and writing. (T. S. Eliot once responded facetiously to a reporter's query about the play he was writing: "Why, you see, in the play I study the relations of certain characters with other characters and of certain characters with themselves.") For some writers, any form can get them going. Prior to beginning *Shadow Train*, John Ashbery decided to "write fifty poems of sixteen lines each, so then I knew what I had to do—right?"

Or, you may want to begin with a plan, such as the two-page scenario Flaubert wrote for *Madame Bovary*. In "The Philosophy of Composition," Poe writes that the author should start with the effect on the reader and plan right through to the dénouement. He claims that before writing "The Raven," he determined it would be about a hundred lines long and require a refrain with a long *o* and an *r* (voilà: *nevermore*). Poe began composing near the end of the poem, "where all works of art should begin." Another writer might not have known there would even be a raven until one came tapping, or what the raven might say until it opened its beak.

Whether you start with an ending or little more than an inkling of a beginning, you should stay open to discoveries along the way. You may find out that you know more than you thought, or that what you thought you knew doesn't hold up to the scrutiny of writing—and you come to know something else.

Originality

If originality is an issue for you, consider W. H. Auden's distinction between *original* and *authentic:* "Some writers confuse authenticity, which they ought always to aim at, with originality, which they should never bother about."

If you do bother about being original, utilize this definition: "Proceeding immediately from its source, or having its source in itself; not arising from or depending on any other thing of the kind; underived, independent." Ask yourself: Did you derive the piece from someone else? Or did it spring up independently?

If the answers are "no" and "yes," then make no apologies. If the answers are "yes" and "no," then you can resort to Ezra Pound's directive and "make it new."

If you can't make it new, make it yours. In Stephen Sondheim's *Sunday in the Park with George,* the painter justifies his artistic drought by asserting he has nothing to say "that's not been said," and his companion counters, "Said by *you?*" This is a mantra to write by.

If you eliminate from contention any material that has been handled admirably by so many others, what's left? Such was the dilemma confronted by French poet-composer Blondel de Nesle in this verse: "There's not a word or verse one can think up any more, / no matter how much one picks and chooses, / that hasn't been said and said again / . . . As for me, I can't keep from singing."

This was composed in the twelfth century: before

Shakespeare, before Blake, before Dickinson, before Joyce, before Wolfe, Woolf, and Wolfe, before you and me.

If you are still afraid of serving up a cliché, we only have to go back to the twentieth century for Pulitzer Prize–winning poet Charles Simic's notebook entry: "The dream of every honest cliché is to enter a great poem." The two key words here are *honest* and *great*. Not easy, but worth aspiring toward.

Within and Without

On a hot summer day, I was standing on the corner of Seventy-Second Street and Broadway in Manhattan. A man in a long black coat ran up to me, stopped short, and implored, "Do you know what happened?"

"Where?" I instinctively replied.

"Anywhere!" he shrieked and ran off.

I assume what he really meant was: "Do you know where to get material for writing?"

"Where?"

"Anywhere."

Your pen or keyboard is the mill, and the whole world is grist. Through writing, you perceive, illuminate, and interpret what goes on internally and externally—as the Beatles sing, "within you and without you." You look for material with your eyes and mind's eye, and listen with your ears and mind's ear. That's the writer's edge: three eyes and three ears.

You can open yourself to the influence of other writers, but you should never forget to look inward as well. In Sir Philip Sidney's sixteenth-century sonnet "Loving in Truth," the poet seeks inspiration by "Oft turning others' leaves, to see if thence would flow / Some fresh and fruitful showers upon my sunburned brain," until "helpless in my throes, / Biting my truant pen" he receives this piece of advice: "'Fool,' said my Muse to me, 'look in thy heart, and write.'"

Write what you know is commonly given advice, and fine advice it is, especially for writers who doubt that anything *they* know could be worth writing about. But don't take this to mean "Don't write what you don't know" or "Only write what you know firsthand."

If I only wrote what I knew firsthand, I would not have written stories from the points of view of an aging ambassador and a touring folk singer; Kafka would not have written *Metamorphosis* or *Amerika* (actually, he didn't—he wrote *The Man Who Disappeared*, which was posthumously named *Amerika* by Max Brod); and Stephen Crane would not have written *The Red Badge of Courage*. Crane eventually did witness real battles, which led him to conclude, with relief, "*The Red Badge* is all right." (If Kafka had made it to the United States, he might have thought otherwise about the accuracy of *Amerika*. *Metamorphosis* is another story.)

Let's amend the adage:

Write what you know; write what you know intuitively; write what you would like to know; write in order to know; write so that the reader may know.

from
Based on a True Life: A Memoir in Pieces

For things that are not known—at least not anymore—and that there is now no way of finding out about, one has to fall back on imagination. This is not the same thing as the truth, but neither is it necessarily a falsehood.
—William Maxwell, *Billy Dyer and Other Stories*

Author's Note: Most names have been changed to protect people from my memory.

The Religion Stories: Message (1951)

My mother and I walk to the synagogue to see Grandpa Popowsky. I am four. She explains that it is against the rules for mommies to go near the grandpas at shul, so I will be the messenger. She hands me a piece of paper and nudges me into the large room.

Men walk about aimlessly, heads bobbing, making strange sounds. The room is crowded but everyone seems alone. When I play make-believe—*vroom vrooming* with a toy car— occasionally I look around to make sure the world is where I left it, but my grandfather doesn't pause, so I tug on his pants.

"*Avram*"—he calls me by my Hebrew name—"is there trouble?" I want to play, too; my mother isn't allowed to pull me away. But I am a good boy and give my grandfather the message. He pats me on the head and resumes his *vrooming*.

Some people have a window of opportunity to find religion: shivering in a battle trench, interpreting a hallucination as a vision, or coming across an injured animal while on the way to jump off a bridge. This may have been my window. If I had climbed through and davened with my grandfather, might I have received a message that would speak to me for the rest of my life?

The Father Stories: Downpours (1953-1996)

My father promises to take me to the Giants game at the Polo Grounds. There are two New York Giants teams, but if you just say *Giants* everyone knows you don't mean the football team. The morning starts dark and gray, and by 11:00 a.m. the downpour is relentless, the kind football teams play in but not baseball teams. My father says we'll go another day.

I protest that it is just a rain delay, and picture everyone sitting around making small talk about the old days, like the announcers do on the radio. I put up such a fuss that my father says he will teach me the lesson that we can't control everything, especially the weather. We drive toward Manhattan silently and a little faster than usual, which I like.

We out-drive the rain, and when we reach the strip of the Major Deegan Expressway where you can see Yankee Stadium out of one window and the Polo Grounds out of the other, my father points out that no one west of St. Louis can see a major league stadium anywhere.

We enter the tunnel to the stands, steps quickening toward the world of the sun-beamed grass, soft brown base paths, bases like clouds, men in white tossing white balls. My father shakes the usher's hand, slipping him some coins; the usher nods and leads us closer to the field.

Forty-three years later, my father is given a terminal diagnosis. I offer to accompany him to his first chemotherapy session. He meets me at the train station, and we drive silently, slower than usual, which I like. It isn't until we are three towns past the doctor's office that I am able to get the words out that he must turn around. This storm cannot be driven through.

Elegy for the Little Man (1953)

One of my classmates has the demeanor of a little man.

In 1953 Brooklyn, boys are required to wear ties to school; most of us have one or two clip-ons, worn until they become invisible. Except for the little man—he has many ties, and they are always perfectly knotted. Each morning after he takes off his coat he pauses at the classroom mirror and adjusts his tie. "Windsor knot," he announces to anyone who stares.

One day, the little man and I stay after school to help the teacher rearrange the bookshelves. It is taking a long time, and I start to toss in the books. The little man says, "My father always says, 'If you are going to do something, get it right.' " I am impressed, and we redo the shelf.

On the first day after Christmas vacation, the teacher— younger than my mother—asks the class to gather in the story area because she has something to tell us. The little man was killed in a car accident over the vacation. She could have told the class he moved away, she says, but she thinks we should always know the truth.

Now a grown man, I can't remember what the little man looked like. But I can picture this vividly: It's a December blizzard night. The little man's family is going visiting. His father is warming up the car. "Hurry up, dear, we're late," his mother says gently as the little man stands, his back to me, at the mirror next to the Christmas tree, getting his Windsor knot just so.

Big
(1954)

Three of us sit on the stoop waiting for the street fight. Not our battle—this one for the younger kids. From the next block comes the screaming swarm, twice as many as the fighters from our block. We look at each other and attack, screaming even louder. "Look out, it's the big kids," someone shouts, and they run off. I will never again feel this big.

Two Science Projects (1958-1960)

Teamwork

Coming up on the deadline for the Science Fair, I have nothing prepared. In desperation, I copy a diagram of the human brain onto a piece of oak-tag, and I tell my mother I am going to make a model out of papier-mâché. She brings home a sheep's brain she got from the butcher. I display it next to the model of the human brain. My table gets the most attention.

Demonstration

I read in a science book about how to spin a copper wheel fueled only by a lightbulb. I meticulously follow the instructions but cannot get it to work. I turn it in anyway, with a short paper about how it works, knowing that it doesn't. The teacher is fascinated and asks me to come up to the front for a demonstration. I plug in the lightbulb, wait for a miracle, and feign shock when nothing happens. The teacher consoles me.

The Religion Stories: Nativity (1959–1963)

Each year, the Village of Lynbrook sets up a crèche on the grass a few blocks from my house. Each year my friend and I rearrange the animals. We have no idea what any of it means.

O How I Loved Before I Knew Lasting Love: Girl from the North Country (1964-1968)

I am smitten with Sara, who has long straight hair, and I get more smitten each time I listen to Dylan's "Girl from the North Country," with her long hair flowing down her breast.

My first date with Sara is to the junior prom. The chartered bus takes the recently repaved road to the beach club, wheels humming over the fresh tar. The sweetness of her shoulder under my arm (I rest my hand on the back of the seat so, technically, I don't have my arm around her—too soon for that), her long hair rolling and flowing down her breast. I wonder if I will get to touch that breast later, after the buses drop us back at the school, when the real partying begins.

But Sara disappears from the after-prom party, rumor has it with Vinnie, a greaser bordering on being a hood from the other side of the Long Island Rail Road tracks. Woozy from cheap screwdrivers, I go home and sleep till noon.

I hear through telephone news that Sara was spotted with Vinnie, who was "pinning her to the backseat" of his car, and the word is that I spent the night drunk in a ditch. I hope that the Sara rumor is as false as the one about me.

Sara calls, gasps she is sorry, her voice torn with hoarseness and tears, confirming the worst when she cries, "Can you ever forgive me? Will you never speak to me again?" I haven't given that a thought but I reply, "No, I will never speak to you again," a pledge I keep for the remainder of the school year.

All summer I yearn for this girl from the north country, reliving my arm draped by her long hair on the bus humming over the fresh tar of the new road, but feel a stab whenever I think of her being pinned to the backseat of Vinnie's car.

In September, Sara is placed in front of me in homeroom, her hair hanging long, inches away. I nod hello, then gradually resume talking to her, trying to impress her by copying chord progressions from *Sing Out* magazine into my notebook or putting checkmarks on music listings in the *Village Voice*.

One day she brushes my hand as we leave the room but doesn't look back. Another day, when the bell rings, she turns around and says, "Oh, Alan, I'm so confused . . . my feelings toward you." Or at least that's what I think she says, but how could that be? I never ask her, never touch the girl from the north country's breast.

A few years later, I hear that Vinnie went to Vietnam and now wears a black glove on his right hand because one of his fingers was blown off. I wonder if it was one of the fingers that helped convince Sara to be pinned to the backseat. I hear that Sara moved to Israel, where she lives on a kibbutz. I replay in my mind, over and over, the words she may have said to me: "Oh, Alan, I'm so confused . . . my feelings toward you."

Yes, she did say it. She did.

The Music Stories: Fun Guy (1965)

If only I could sing, I would be such a fun guy. I wouldn't have to sing really well, just well enough to belt out a song at a party, with more bravado than bravura. And everyone would stop talking and sing along with me, then slap my back and say, "Hey, you know, that was *fun*."

Or, when dating someone for the first time, joking across Fifty-Seventh Street after a movie, I would stop her in front of the invisible Steinway showroom window, put my arm around her playfully, and do a couple choruses of "Let Me Call You Sweetheart," miming the piano accompaniment with my free hand. Then I'd sing something silly, like, to the tune of "They Tried to Tell Us We're Too Young": "They tried to sell us egg foo young . . ." And she would laughingly throw her arms around me and think *what a fun guy*. I'd also show her, and this is crucial, that I know when to stop.

I'd sing lullabies to friends' babies, and tasteful tunes, on request, after weddings and funerals. On snowy nights by the fire with someone I really care for, I'd play my guitar and whisper-sing a warming love song—"Time after Time" comes to mind—remembering, of course, when to stop.

I wouldn't deluge or delude myself with the notion: *Maybe if I did some voice training I could be on stage!* No, I'd be content to confine my modest talent to social singing, saving my fantasies for the shower, where I'd be Sinatra at Carnegie, Aznavour in a saloon.

As it is, I'm not even good enough for the shower. I offend my own sensibilities. I'd have to take a plane, train, and cab to arrive in the neighborhood of a melody, where I'd soon get lost.

I've been told that anyone can sing. Perhaps, but the odds against you are prohibitive when your natural equipment is woefully deficient and any potential for vocal cord refinement was stunted by years of not even trying. What happened was this:

My grade-school music teacher picked all but five in my class to be in the chorus. The remaining atonal quintet was given the class newspaper to keep us busy while the others prepared for the Fall Concert, Christmas Recital, and Spring Show. Which is why I stopped trying to sing, but can write this.

Still, I grew to love music in high school, especially folk and blues. I learned to play the guitar, though I couldn't tune it very well. "Close enough for folk music," I'd announce after spending minutes tightening and loosening strings. I'd accompany friends on the guitar at informal hoots, but the singers would have more fun.

A guy in Washington Square Park led me through the folk guitarist's initiatory rite by teaching me "Freight Train" in the key of C. And on the beach at Newport between sessions of the Folk Festival, a guitarist from Cambridge—who claimed to have dated Jim Kweskin's sister—taught me how to keep a double bass line when fingerpicking. This resulted in an extra layer to my playing, leading to my first falsetto "whoo!" response two months later at a party. My most proud moment was when someone referred to me as a "blues guitarist." When I listened to Bob Dylan and Pete Seeger records, I'd think:

"I bet if it hadn't been for that music teacher I could sing as well as they do."

Before I leave for college, one of my teachers advises students to take advantage of the clean slate we'll have in a new place, enabling us to break bad behavior patterns and start new, good ones. No one would know any better and respond, "Who are you trying to kid?" During orientation week I become the kind of guy who initiates conversations with "How ya doin'?" instead of waiting to be chosen. I get elected to the student council and am rushed by three fraternities.

I have gotten good on the guitar, and as word spreads about my prowess, other guitarists start appearing at my door: "Hey, you the cat with the Harmony Sovereign? Wanna check out my Gibson?"

Peculiarly, one afternoon in my dorm room I take this to mean that now I can sing. I am playing alone, doing my instrumental "House of the Rising Sun," a combination of the Dylan and Van Ronk arrangements. I pick up steam, really cooking, and some guys gather around. I start humming, then singing under the guitar. It sounds all right. What I lack in tone I make up for with passionate growling and nasal twanging. I sing gradually louder, amazed at how good it sounds. The long rest has done my vocal cords good. That music teacher just couldn't hear the potential.

I finish with a guitar run that isn't Dylan or Van Ronk, and as the resolving chord resounds I wait for the chorus of "whoo"s. One of the freshmen says, "Man, you play a hell of a guitar, but you sure have one weird voice." Another says something about a tortured cat. They all laugh. Finally, someone says, "How much you want for that guitar?"

This episode shuts me up once again, allowing my vocal cords to continue their withering journey to atrophy. But, for a few minutes there, I was a real fun guy, and it will remain the barometer by which I measure happiness.

The Father Stories: First Mention (1967)

My father often makes snorting sounds, brushes his chin against his shoulder, taps our knees or arms while talking to us. The word *twitch* is not used until a friend from college visits and says, "I noticed your father has a twitch." I act as if I know all about it, no big deal, and I change the subject.

Stool Pigeon
(1969)

I get a temp job on Manhattan's diamond block, Forty-
Seventh between Sixth and Seventh, sitting in an upstairs
room, transporting gems from various bins into various
envelopes. It is menial, minimum wage. The perk for me is
spending my lunch hour across the street at the Gotham
Book Mart; I can see the *Wise Men Fish Here* sign from my
window.

The woman sitting next to me has concentration camp
numbers tattooed on her bulky arm. A young man around my
age sits on the other side. He asks me to join him for lunch
and tells me that he has been watching everything for a while
and has determined that the managers do not know exactly
what they have until we sort the gems; how easy it would be
to slip a few in our pockets. He proposes that we take turns
on lookout duty. I decline.

That afternoon, one of the bosses comes over to the
young man, says, "Can I talk to you for a minute?" and
escorts him out of the room. I never see him again. To this
day, he must believe that I ratted him out.

Young Asses
(1969)

In the autumn of 1969, Alicia and I jam into a VW microbus with some of her Goddard friends to tour the leaf-draped Vermont countryside. Most of the others are stoned and gush about the fall leaves ("it's like swimming in a pond with candy fish everywhere").

Driving (and not under the influence) is Ernie, pudgy, pushing the don't-trust age of thirty, one of the progressive teachers at the progressive college Alicia attends. He pulls over occasionally to take photographs with his vintage Leica that he doesn't let anyone touch (in direct violation of the spirit of the times).

"You two," he says to Alicia and me while the others are off somewhere swimming with the candy fish, "do me a favor and take off your clothes and walk up that path holding hands. The light is perfect, the leaves are peak. It'll be a great photograph. I'll only shoot from the back, no one will know it's you."

Alicia says yes, I say no, equally uncomfortable about walking around naked as about Ernie seeing Alicia naked, even from the back. I don't want her in his head and in the heads of everyone who would see the picture.

Ernie and Alicia coax me, but I continue to refuse, just like I refused the pot I was offered before we left.

When Alicia is long gone from my life, I will wish I had said yes, so I could watch my past walking away, our young asses against a backdrop of candy leaves.

Once a Year
(1970)

While working on the Binghamton Evening Press, right out of college, I am trying to decide whether to leave the job, as I have planned, at the end of the summer, or to stay indefinitely.

I am sitting at my desk when the assistant city editor walks by and says, "See you after my vacation." I tell him to have a good time, and I resume writing.

Not long after, I look up and he is walking by me again. "I thought you were on vacation?" I say.

"I was, for two weeks."

"Where'd you go?"

"My driveway. I've been wanting to repave it for a couple of years. I got a lot of other things done around the house, and played some tennis. Yeah, that's it till next year."

"That sounds nice," I say, my mind made up.

Young Screams
(1973)

I am working nights as a machine operator, recently out of a six-year relationship with Alicia, having some dark nights of the soul. So I am excited when someone in my poetry workshop tells me about Jeremy, a Jungian analyst who may lower his rates for a poet. I can tell everyone I am in Jungian analysis in order to mine my unconscious for poetry.

Jeremy's office is on Fifth Avenue near Eleventh Street, the heart of Jungian country. He is in his midthirties, with curly, longish dark hair, wearing dark-green corduroy pants and a black turtleneck. Jeremy asks me a few questions, ending with "What are you afraid of?" I shock myself with the answer: "I'm afraid I am going to start twitching, like my father." He agrees to take me on at a reduced rate, then mentions that our sessions will be interrupted in a month by a trip to Zurich to meet with his mentor.

Jung. Zurich. Fifth Avenue. Unconscious. Dreams. Oh, how the words roll off my young-poet tongue.

I start having more interesting dreams, perhaps to please Jeremy:

I am a shrimp in lobster sauce. The lobster sauce fills the Fillmore East on Second Avenue, and all the concert-goers are shrimps. Two of the other shrimps are engaged in deep conversation. I recognizes one as being the rock critic for the Village Voice. *I am envious of the shrimp talking to him.*

I am in hell, protesting that I have been unfairly placed here. I am assigned to give a talk on misery, and am in a panic because I feel inadequate to the task.

I look in the freezer, which turns into a giant room. There's something wrapped in tinfoil. I unwrap it. It is me.

I am a guest on The Tonight Show, *and I am killing. I ad-lib one line that brings the house down, and has Johnny banging on his desk for mercy: "You could get a job as a store display in a Jell-O factory."*

My writing cupboard is newly stocked with surrealistic images that I cook into my poems, and I start to feel better about myself. I miss Jeremy the two weeks he is in Zurich, but enjoy saying, "My Jungian analyst is in Zurich with his mentor."

Our mutual friend invites me to a party, warning me that Jeremy may be there. The party is loud and crowded, with people dancing to Motown in one room and mingling in another. As I stand in the hallway between the two rooms, coming on to a woman, Jeremy—hair unkempt, wearing a flowered shirt— dances by, lips in a pout and fists circling in a "do the monkey" motion. "Hey," Jeremy says as he shimmies by.

"Who was *that?*" the woman asks.

"That's my Jungian analyst," I answer with pride. "His mentor is in Zurich."

The next week, at the end of our session, Jeremy asks me to move from the couch to the chair for a few minutes, he has something to tell me. I am afraid the ride is over; I'm not crazy or interesting enough.

"I am ending my practice, as it is now," Jeremy declares solemnly. He has been going through some heavy changes personally and professionally. He can't, in good faith, continue to do Jungian analysis. "I've rented a loft on Spring Street, and I am changing to primal scream therapy."

Jeremy offers to refer me to another Jungian, or I can make the change with him. In college, I was intrigued by primal scream and other fringe treatments. A motto of the left is *If you're not part of the solution, you're part of the problem,* and many believe that the likes of Arthur Janov and R. D. Laing are part of the solution. I'm no longer active politically, so this would make me less of a problem. I can have interesting dreams on my own, but I need help to scream.

"I'm with you," I declare. "What does your mentor in Zurich think about this?"

"He thinks I'm crazy," Jeremy says. I wait for him to smile but he doesn't.

Two weeks later I have my first session in Jeremy's Spring Street loft, with peeling walls, no couch, no desk. A large portion of the floor is covered with a tattered wrestling mat, pillows scattered around. "Lie down, get comfortable," Jeremy says, and we begin our transition from talk therapy to pretalk therapy.

Jeremy sits next to me in the lotus position, and I turn sideways to face him, head pedestaled on my hand. We talk for a while about my dreams, then Jeremy asks me to lie flat on my back and make various noises. "Good, now let the pillows have it." I punch the pillows around but feel limp and spiritless at the end of the session. "It'll take some getting used to," Jeremy says, his hand on my shoulder.

After a few sessions, I am screaming my head off and beating the crap out of the pillows. I am on the cutting edge.

Spring Street. Primal Scream. I can't wait for Jeremy to guide me back to infancy so I can curdle my blood with transcendent shrieks.

At one session, while lying on the mat for the ever-briefer talk segment, I mention my difficulty expressing anger.

"Let's wrestle," Jeremy says.

"Let's what?"

"Wrestle. Let's see what happens."

Jeremy is two inches shorter than I but powerfully built, muscles rippling through his T-shirt. I am a runner, in every sense of the word. But I am also a gamer. "Okay," I say.

Jeremy reaches his arms around my chest and rolls me over. I halfheartedly fight back and am surprised that I am able to spin Jeremy around. But each time Jeremy is relocated, he regains control. Jeremy is toying with me, and I feel silly but don't know what to do. After all, Jeremy is my primal scream *née* Jungian therapist on the cutting edge on Spring Street.

Jeremy shoves me off balance and pins my right wrist with his left knee. Just as Jeremy's right knee approaches my left wrist, I realize that Jeremy is going to hold me down until I scream bloody hell. I picture myself frozen in tinfoil. I remember Babes beating up that kid in third grade. I'm with my grandfather in shul. I am in free fall to the cradle. I bolt.

My surge turns Jeremy over and I pounce on top of him. Jeremy smiles and motions *surrender.* My adrenaline gauge zags toward empty, and I flop onto my back, breathing heavily but deeply.

"You fought back," Jeremy says. "Why didn't you fight back sooner?"

"Because only a sadist would hurt someone who doesn't fight back."

"How badly did you really think you could get hurt? And how did you know you couldn't win?"

"I get it. I should send those poems out, ask those women out." I am pumped, my elation gauge zigs, but quickly zags back when I realize, "Someone else might have *really* hurt me."

Jeremy tilts his head forward.

"I guess I have to know *when* to take risks," I say.

Jeremy grins and says he'll see me next week.

At the start of the next session, Jeremy tells me of another change in his practice. "It's really hard to do this, one-to-one, in New York City." Jeremy has bought a rundown house in the country. His clients will come for marathon group sessions. They will paint, do carpentry, and cook. Janov meets Laing.

I tell Jeremy I'll think about it, and we shake hands. But I have gotten as close to the edge as I can for now, and I can't risk falling off. I will never see Jeremy again.

Overtime
(1975)

In my first full year of teaching I follow the advice an actor friend was given: "Never say no to a job when you're starting out." Everything blooms at once. I am getting residencies from Teachers & Writers, Poets in the Schools, and Poets & Writers, while teaching as an adjunct at Bronx Community College. At each new school I have to prove myself. I have no backlog of assignments to pull out of the bag, so I am constantly preparing while doing my own writing. My toughest session is on Saturday mornings at Bronx Community College, a remedial writing class that meets from 8:00 a.m. till noon.

One Friday, starting my fourth and last class of the day, I open my mouth and realize I don't have enough left in me to go through with my plan. I am incapable of jumping around the room trying to excite poetry out of the kids. In desperation, I ask them what's important enough for them to write about. It turns out to be my best session of the week, opening up a whole new avenue of teaching. I leave elated but still exhausted; Saturday in the Bronx looms.

At 7:00 a.m. I somehow find myself climbing up the hill to the Bronx Community College campus. The stores are closed and the sky is gray with an early-winter bite. I can't remember turning off the alarm. What if I am dreaming that I am on my way to school, but I am really in bed about to miss my class? I don't know which is more terrifying: if I shake myself real hard and come awake in my bed, or if

I don't. I shudder, but just feel more fuzzy. I must assume this is real and continue to slog up the hill.

By the time class starts, I am sure I am barely awake. I plunge into comma splices and subject-verb agreement without using those terms. As usual, Patterson comes in thirty minutes late; Patterson is an overnight conductor on the D-train and insists on going home and changing into a suit before coming to class—he'd rather be late than unkempt. Like many of my other students, he is well past college age, taking advantage of the City University's open admissions policy.

During a break, I find Ignacio waiting for me in the hallway. Ignacio has three kids and a full-time job, and took remedial writing before but failed because a crisis at home forced him to miss the last few classes. "Professor, I was here on time," Ignacio says. (I have asked the students to call me Alan, but some insist on calling me professor—they have enough Alans in their lives, they need a professor or two.) "Then I went to the john just to close my eyes for a few minutes, and I just woke up."

"Okay," I say, gesturing toward the classroom. The exhaustion hits me again. I have to go to the bathroom, but I am afraid that if I sit down, I too will fall asleep. I head back into the room.

After class, three students wait for me in the hallway, but they are blocked by Iris, a nurse in her fifties. "Alan," she says, "go home to your bed."

O How I Loved Before I Knew Lasting Love: The Interview (1975)

I have been asked to apply for a full-time college teaching job. I am underpublished but am the choice of the outgoing writer. They send a student from the search committee to my apartment. Maggie has long blonde hair and is beautiful. I tell myself to keep my eye on the job, but I can't keep my eyes off of her.

We talk for two hours and I offer to walk her to the subway. We reach the Eighty-Sixth Street station but keep walking, past 79, 72, 66, 59, 50, 42, 34, 28, 23, 18, and 14. Maggie asks a lot of questions along the way. When we reach the building where she is staying on Tenth Street—in an apartment once occupied by Marlon Brando—she invites me up and says, "I hope you realize the interview was over hours ago and you don't have to answer my questions."

In bed, she tells me she is having an affair with the married writer who encouraged me to apply for the job. We agree not to have sex until she breaks it off with him, and we fall asleep. At 4:00 a.m. I awaken to see her staring at me. "Who are you, Alan Ziegler?" she says sweetly, and I am convinced she will help me find out.

The next afternoon, she calls to tell me that she learned that the dean hired someone a couple of days ago but didn't tell the search committee. I think: Maybe she knew this yesterday, maybe she didn't. Maybe there really was a search committee, maybe there wasn't. Maybe the married writer set this up, maybe he didn't. (In a few weeks—when we are deep into our relationship—he will call me in the middle of the night to sing me a love song he has written for Maggie and tell me he is not mad at me even though "I really loved her—I even stopped *shtupping* other students for her.")

The story goes on for two years, but I have told the best part.

Anywhere
(1975)

On Seventy-Second Street and Broadway in July, a man in a long black coat comes running to me, desperation in his eyes. "Do you know what happened?" he implores.

"Where?" I ask.

The man pauses and looks at me as if I have asked a naive question. "*Any*where!" he shrieks and runs off, before I can think of an answer.

I am making a list, should I run into him again.

Friendship and Art (1977)

The buzzer rings near midnight. It is Robert, distraught. He has had a fight with his girlfriend and walked out. Can he stay with me?

Sure, I say, and put on some tea. I really don't want to deal with this, but you don't turn the lovelorn away from your door.

We talk for a while. It sounds like a flare-up, and I suggest that Robert go back and try to work things out before they get worse. He leaves, and when I next see him, he says everything is all right. I feel good about helping to save a relationship.

Robert and I gradually drop out of touch. Two years later I run into him on the subway. He tells me he is back in school and is writing poems. He asks if I want to see one, and pulls a sheaf of typed poems from his book bag. He shuffles through the pages and hands me one.

As I read I realize it is about that night. I am portrayed as a cold person who barely tolerates the intrusion and says good-sounding things only to get rid of him.

"What do you think?" Robert asks, as if the poem were about roses in winter.

"It's nice," I reply, the words you use when you want to break a poet's spirit.

O How I Found Lasting Love Because Art Forgets to Leave His Keys in the Car on Martha's Vineyard
(1980-1986)

Because Art forgets to leave his keys in the car, Gay can't drive me to the airport on Martha's Vineyard.

Because Gay can't drive me, we walk to the airport, a long shot to make the plane, but we can always get langoustines at the airport café.

Because we walk, a neighbor driving her daughter Beth to the same flight sees us and gives us a ride.

Because I meet Beth, we wait for the plane together—the whole two hours that it is delayed.

Because we have a couple of drinks at the bar and a couple of complimentary drinks on the plane, I overcome my shyness and ask Beth for her phone number.

Because I am sober 99 percent of the time, I don't call her.

Because I run into Beth on the street weeks later, she tells me, "It is so gratuitous running into you," and invites me to a party at her apartment.

Because I go to Beth's party, I become infatuated with one of her roommates, Meredith, a singer from Traverse City, Michigan.

Because I get involved with Meredith (and that's a whole other story) I go with her to Traverse City and she takes me to the Interlochen Arts Academy campus. I see the showcase of visiting writers, and Meredith says, "Why don't you get a job as writer in residence here and we can live together for the term?"

Because Meredith said that, I apply for—and get—the writer in residence job at Interlochen; with it comes a cabin with a fireplace.

Because Meredith and I break up, I find myself alone at Interlochen and become friends with Clara, who soon moves to New York.

Because Clara moves to New York, when I return home she introduces me to her friend Jen, and Jen and I become friends.

Because Jen decides to go camping one Saturday, she calls on Friday to cancel our date to a jazz club later that night and, as an afterthought, perhaps so I won't feel rejected (even though we are not romantically involved), she asks me to join her at an early-evening Christmas-season party.

Because I go to the party, I am introduced to Erin who, it turns out, lives around the corner from me.

Because I am introduced to Erin, we fall in love and get married.

love at first sight

The Stories Could Have Ended Here (1981)

On my first morning in the Interlochen cabin, I light the oven with a match. It goes out, and I light it again. I go into the other room to empty my bag and hear an explosion. I turn to see the oven door being flung open. A wine bottle in the sink shatters.

The Religion Stories: Grace under Fire (1984)

I meet Erin at a Christmas party, and we get serious quickly. Erin comes from a devoutly religious family. Her father, Paul, is a church organist, composer of liturgical music, and music school dean, and Erin has always sung in a church choir. She doesn't have a problem with my being Jewish—she dated a rabbi for a while—but it does bother her that I am not religious.

When it looks possible that we may be spending the rest of our lives together, Erin starts to feel troubled about the eternity dilemma. Erin hasn't been brought up to think that Jews go to hell, but she does believe that devotion to Jesus will result in a heavenly eternity with God, His son, and His followers. She isn't *sure* that non-Christians will be excluded, but even the possibility of spending our mortal lives together only to be separated for eternity scares the hell out of her.

The subject comes to a head one night at a restaurant. We become engaged in a discussion more serious than any previous political, artistic, or social deliberation I have ever been part of. I am arguing for my life: if I cannot convince Erin that we won't be separated for eternity, I might lose her for the only chunk of time I can count on.

I am good at debating, but can my persuasive skills counter Erin's faith? How can I even fathom what she is feeling? I remember my mother's father davening, and I try to put myself into his skin. I feel a moment of clarity, fusing logic with a feeling I have never quite had before, a feeling I can only denote as faith, which I try to express to Erin:

"It doesn't make sense," I say, "that God would exclude good people from heaven. It makes even less sense that God would punish you forever because I don't believe in Jesus Christ." I realize that at some point I have stopped *not* believing in God, though I still don't *believe*. I am becoming an agnostic, which I previously thought was reserved for those without the guts to come out and say they are atheists.

I now have utter faith that if there *is* a God, He will do right by Erin and me. And Erin comes to have faith in that, too.

My first dinner with Erin's parents. After the food is on the table, her father asks if I would mind if they did the blessing. I say okay, that we sometimes do that with my family: my father asks someone to say *grace*, I say "grace," and we eat.

Erin's father takes her right hand with his left, Erin takes her mother's hand, and her mother, Esther, offers her hand to me. I take it, and complete the chain by grasping Paul's right hand. We bow our heads while he recites: "Heavenly Father, accept our thanks for this food and for all of Thy blessings. In Jesus Christ's name we pray. Amen."

The word *Jesus* comes as a jolt, and I recoil when Erin's parents squeeze my hands as they repeat "Amen."

I freeze inside. I don't mind saying grace, I don't mind holding hands, but I do mind the invocation of Jesus while holding hands. I feel like I have been manipulated into the first step of a conversion protocol.

I don't say anything to Erin until after her parents leave, and then I let it out. She says she understands my discomfort and assures me there is no plan afoot to bring me into the fold. She wonders how long I will be mad at her carelessness and how long she'll "have to pay for this."

"My God," I reply, "what have those other men done to you?" and I hug her.

The next time we have dinner together, Paul says they'll skip the blessing, but I hold my hands out and ask him to please go on. We all take hands and Paul says: "Heavenly Father, accept our thanks for this food and for all of thy blessings. Take care of our loved ones," we pray.

And I squeeze hands and say "Amen," feeling devoutly faithful to those at the table.

On the Road to Lee (1991–1993)

Nick loves to drive and doesn't mind going out of his way—he once drove from New Orleans to Tallahassee to have lunch with a friend. I am going to visit him at Interlochen, and he tells me about a low fare to Grand Rapids, offering to pick me up at the airport. My plane arrives an hour late, and I meet Nick at the bar.

We have been driving for about an hour when I ask him how much farther. He says it is another hour and a half. Nick is spending five hours in the car just to pick up a friend at the airport; he's not the only one who would do that, but few do it as naturally.

There are hardly any other cars on the highway, with darkness on either side, and many miles between exits that lead to deeper darkness. We pass a sign for *Lee: One Mile*.

"Have you ever been to Lee?" I ask.

"Never heard of it," Nick says.

About a minute later we whiz past a hitchhiker. "Did you see that guy?" I ask.

"Yeah, who'd stop here? I'd stop. But I'm not going to back up on this road."

"How the hell did he get that far, and no farther?"

"Guess his last ride was turning off at Lee."

"Or he's from Lee."

We say it simultaneously: "He *is* Lee."

Lee becomes our code word for anyone physically or emotionally adrift in the world.

A couple of years later, Nick and I converge in Tallahassee, where we stay with Frank and Helen, watching movies late into the night on their VCR. Helen's college-age son and two female friends stay over one night. Nick sleeps on the living room floor, and I on the couch. After we go to bed, each of the kids takes a shower—tiptoeing past us to and from the bathroom. Early the next morning, they repeat the ritual. Six showers, twelve tiptoeings past us. "They're the cleanest kids in the world," Nick says to me.

After my visit, I am to take a bus to Jacksonville, from where I will fly to New York. Nick drives me to the Tallahassee bus terminal. Until the bus actually pulls out, I think Nick may change his mind and drive me to the Jacksonville airport and hang out with me until my 8:00 a.m. flight. But Nick looks tired. As the bus pulls out, I shiver in the backseat. Three soldiers loudly flirt with a young woman, but when she tells them that her fiancé is stationed at their base, they settle into a round of "do-you-know?" I feel obligated to listen carefully to their rhythms of speech and turns of phrases, but I am tired and just want them to shut up. I realize that Nick and I are starting to get a little old, and I feel a pang of terror.

The bus station in Jacksonville is bright and busy at 3:00 a.m. I walk around, squinting in the fluorescent glare, picturing myself in forty years a lunatic roaming Broadway babbling about how the general downfall has been caused by fluorescent lighting.

A couple dozen guys are hanging around, looking like a casting call for a grade-B thriller set in a Southern town where a New York Jew is stranded and terrorized. Looking for a taxi, I pass a vending machine. I never eat candy bars, but the Nestlé's Crunch looks awfully good so I eat one and buy one for later. I find the taxi stand, where three guys are playing cards. When I ask if I can get a cab to a motel near the airport, one smiles and says, "It's my turn; I got this one."

I realize why he was so eager for the fare when we are going 70 on a highway, darkness completely around us, the meter clicking a steady staccato, up to $45 before I see the first glimmer of man-made light—a motel. The driver pulls over.

"Where's the airport?"

"Oh, it's around the bend a ways. The motel will take you there."

I give him three twenties, which he stuffs with magician's speed into his pocket. I don't get a chance to ask for change. The cab screeches away and I walk up the path to the motel. By the time I see the *No Vacancy* sign, the cab's rear lights are extinguished by distance.

The lobby is locked. I toss my bag over my shoulder and return to the highway. A cool drizzle starts. How far is the bend? How long is a "ways"?

The rain feels refreshing after the stuffy bus. The airport can't be too far away. A few stars make pinholes of light through a clearing patch on the horizon. I remember the Nestlé's Crunch, and take small bites as I walk. It tastes even better than the last one.

I hear the roar of a car. I turn around and squint at the brights. I wave. The car doesn't even slow down.

I have become Lee, and it isn't so bad.

The Father Stories: Second Mention (1996)

He sits at the kitchen table, the night before the CAT scan. I notice a note on a piece of scrap paper from a Las Vegas hotel: "What will be? Have I waited too long?" He takes out an issue of *Parade* magazine, which gets bundled with the Sunday paper, and asks me to read an article without saying anything until I am finished. The article is headlined, "Why Is This Happening," and the pull quote at the top is: "Individuals with Tourette's syndrome struggle daily with uncontrollable twitches, vocal outbursts, and painful social embarrassment."

I've heard of Tourette's—but only about people cursing inappropriately. The article is about a baseball player with Tourette's who says, "Mostly I would grunt and clear my throat. Next, my head and neck began to jerk." Tourette's wasn't diagnosed until he was twenty-three.

"I've never known what to call it," my father says. "If this doesn't go well, I wanted you to know it has a name."

The Spare Change Stories (1964-1998)

As a lifelong New Yorker, I've had an extensive but not deeply examined relationship with panhandlers. In the 1960s they were commonly known as bums or derelicts, and most had a story to sell for a quarter; sometimes my spare change bought me valuable cultural information. I heard it first from a panhandler in Times Square that *bad* means *good* (though it took me a while to figure that one out). Another told me about his old friend Billie Holiday and a pair of shoes he once bought her. I was about to buy him a drink when he mentioned his other friend, "That trumpet player, you know who I mean: *Billy Eckstine*." I thought: Everyone knows that Eckstine was a vocalist, not a trumpet player, and I moved on. I found out later that Billy Eckstine started out as a trumpet player in Harlem and hung out with Billie Holiday (who, I imagine, one day got a pair of shoes from a friend). I could have gotten a lot more for my quarter.

Here's a story I tell a lot: "There was this bum asleep under a tree in Washington Square Park. I quietly put half of my corned beef sandwich next to him and waited for him to wake up. I didn't want any thanks, but I did want to see the look on his face. He unwrapped the sandwich, peeked under the bread, and scowled. He reached into his coat pocket and pulled out a jar of mustard." (Everyone enjoys the story, though no one believes it's true. It is. As far as I know.)

Living on the Upper West Side in the 1970s, I became familiar with disturbed people roaming Broadway, many of them having been dumped from state mental hospitals when the courts decided that people of no imminent danger to themselves or others could not remain institutionalized. Some seemed to lack the skills to panhandle, including one gaunt man in his thirties who wore a gabardine trench coat no matter the temperature, skulking from block to block and store to store. He would disappear during the winter and somehow reappear—a harbinger of spring.

In the 1980s, there were street people who were not bums or crazies: some of them were apparently victims of the Reagan Administration systematically denying Social Security disability claims. My mother, with advanced cancer, was turned down; we kept appealing until she "won," a month after she died. In her memory, I often gave to beggars who appeared sick or disabled.

In the 1990s, while walking from my apartment on 104th Street up to Columbia, I often felt among the familiar faces of a small town. On the corner of Broadway and 106th Street one man would say over and over, "Spare-some-change-appreciate-it?" in one William-Carlos-Williamsian American beat. A few times I saw him give money to someone even less fortunate. On 107th and Broadway, the guy with the brown corduroy jacket would chant: "Spare some change for a cup of caw*feee?*" Once, I handed him my container of coffee. He smiled and toasted me with it.

One summer afternoon, the sky blackened instantaneously and rain came down in torrents, sending people scurrying for shelter. I wound up sharing an awning with three street people, including one I hadn't seen before. One of the familiar faces said to the newcomer, "I haven't seen you around here. What's your name?" "Eddie," the newcomer replied." "What's your last name?" "Oh, I lost that a long time ago."

One can't give to everyone, all the time. "I'm sorry I can't give you anything," I said once, and the man's face ballooned with rage. "Don't you ever, *ever* say you're sorry for me." At the other end of the spectrum: A young man asked for money, saying he hates himself for asking. He looked healthy, but it was freezing and I could only imagine what it would feel like to be sentenced to an outside prison. I gave him a dollar and he said nothing but followed me as I walked away. I turned around, and he implored: "You're not angry at me, are you?"

Sometimes I'd go for days or weeks without giving anything, partly so I wouldn't have to decide who gets and who doesn't. I reached the point where I didn't feel bad about not giving but always felt good—for a few seconds—when I did.

Then on a frigid night I met my match:

A guy on Broadway and 115th Street asks if I can help him out, and I give him a quarter. He thanks me and holds out three subway tokens, asking me to buy them. "People give me tokens, but I got no place to go. I need to buy food." I excavate the crumpled bills and change in my pocket and separate four singles and two quarters. I give him the money and he spots a ten still in my hand. Without giving me the three tokens, he says, "Let me have the ten and I'll give you more tokens."

Why not? I give him the ten, but he still doesn't give me any tokens. "Thank you," he says. "You're a good man."

"What about the tokens?"

"Oh, no, you said you were giving me a gift."

I get furious and sputter for my money back, but he keeps shaking his head. Finally, I say, "Look, just give me back the ten. Keep the rest of the money."

"I'm sorry, I just can't do that," he says, clutching my money.

My blood rushes to my face, and I snarl, "Then I'm just going to have to get a cop. Do you want all that trouble?"

"You do what you have to do. But I just can't give you this money back. I just can't do that."

I walk away, getting some satisfaction that he might be afraid for a while that I *am* getting a cop. When I calm down, I realize that if I had—out of largesse—*given* him $15 right off, I would be feeling pretty good about myself. Upon examination, it may be that the one common denominator whenever I give a handout is that I maintain the upper hand.

But tonight, for a few minutes, I skulk down Broadway cold, angry, and broke.

The Father Stories: Tough Question (1999)

All night, my father and I avoid talking of the relapse, the upcoming treatment and surgery decisions, the dying dog, what to do with the house. We talk sports at the diner (where he calls the man in the gray suit who welcomes us, "Boss") and the latest developments on the TV shows I watch because he does. I try again to sell him on email, and this time he is receptive; he feels left out of all the communication going on among his children.

We get to the train station a few minutes early and stand at the bottom of the perpetually paralyzed escalator. "This is probably not the time to talk about it," he says, and I stiffen at what he might have been holding back all night.

"Go ahead, I can always take the next train."

"What is the Internet?"

The Father Stories: Inaction (2001)

In the hospital elevator, after the confirming diagnosis, down to the ground floor, the door won't open. "Al, do something," he implores. I push buttons randomly and the door opens. A doctor gets on, nodding as we flee.

I did something, we got out. There's nothing I can do.

The Father Stories: Observation Deck (1989)

My father is claustrophobic. He hardly ever has to be in an enclosed space—except airplanes, but he loves to fly, connecting more to the open sky than to the confinement of the cabin. For a pick-me-up, instead of going to a bar, sometimes he drives to the airport and watches planes take off. He calls it "sniffing the planes."

Since my mother died, my father occasionally takes the Long Island Rail Road and meets me at Penn Station. We have an early lunch at a coffee shop named Andrews on Thirty-Fifth Street, where the waiters and waitresses are nice, even if they rarely get my father's toast dark the way he asks for it. It's enough that occasionally one will ask, "Is it dark enough for you?" He got upset with a new waitress because she didn't seem to care when he pointed out how light the toast was. When we asked for the check, we realized she hardly spoke English. My father left a big tip.

After lunch we walk through Macy's and look at VCRs. My father has shopped for a VCR for a year. By the time the one he's had his eye on goes on sale, a new model with new features has arrived, and he figures he'll wait until the new one goes on sale. Finally I buy him one for Christmas, and after a few phone calls to me for tech support, he tells me he doesn't know how he lived without it.

Usually I am the one who buys something at Macy's— a sweater, or some aftershave with the free gift of a duffel bag or soccer ball. Occasionally I want something more extravagant—a portable CD player or an electronic organizer, anything new on the market—but I don't purchase it until after I put my father on the train.

From Macy's we walk the streets, window-shopping, father and son flaneurs, and wind up at the food plaza on the top floor of the new A&S. We look out over Father & Son Shoes on Sixth Avenue as we sip coffee for an hour or so, until he catches the last train before the peak rush-hour fare kicks in and competition is fiercer for a seat. I can never get much out of him about his past. Mostly we talk about sports and television, and we occasionally spar a few rounds on politics, which sometimes gets out of hand but always ends with a hug before he gets on the train.

One crystallized early spring day, we stop outside of Madison Square Garden to listen to a middle-aged trombone player and his preteen, banjo-playing, tap-dancing son. A Suit with a walkie-talkie confers with them and points toward the edge of Madison Square Garden's property.

"Why is he kicking them out? Doesn't he have anything better to do?" I say to my father.

I gear up for a contretemps on corporate autonomy versus free expression—with my father taking the corporate side, even though he's worn a blue collar all his life—but he replies, "They weren't hurting anybody," as the father and son pack up their instruments.

Buoyed by our rare solidarity against the system, I suggest something I've been wanting to do for months: "Let's get away from it all and go to the top of the Empire State Building."

"I was there yesterday," my father says, his stock answer when he doesn't want something. ("You want to try my calamari?" "Nah, I had some yesterday.") I am forty-two, as old as my father was when I was eighteen, which was when my father stopped calling my shots. Now it is time for the child to be father to the man. "We'll be closer to the airplanes," I persist, and take his arm.

As soon as we enter the elevator, I realize I've made a cruel mistake. I've been picturing the living room–size elevator at the World Trade Center, forgetting that the Empire State Building's elevator is the size of a large closet. Before I can ask my father if he wants to leave, tourists pack in with shopping bags and cameras. The only way not to make physical contact with a stranger is to stand absolutely straight.

My father and I are at attention, pinned to the back, as the doors close. Above the door are lights for each floor up to 20, with the next light indicating the eighty-sixth-floor observation deck. A minute after 20 winks at us, my father mutters something; instead of asking him to repeat it, I pretend I didn't hear him.

When we exit, my father says, "It was a little rough there for a while. I couldn't tell if we were moving." Unsaid is that we will soon have to get back into that elevator.

I have been doing biofeedback exercises, aimed at reducing the body's anxiety arousal by breathing deeply and slowly. I explain this to my father and demonstrate how to breathe from the diaphragm, narrating: "Hold your stomach and feel it move as you breathe in for a count of four; hold your breath for one count, and let it out for another count of four as you feel your diaphragm contract. Hold for a count and repeat."

"You know," I add, "when I was in elementary school, a nurse came to teach us how to brush our teeth—'be sure to spit out, otherwise you just move the germs around'—but no one taught us how to breathe. And wouldn't you say *that's* elementary?"

My father seems distracted as I talk to him, probably thinking about the return elevator trip. He is not one to go for faddish solutions, so I mention that the Chinese knew about breathing thousands of years ago, but I don't press the issue. For now, we are at the top. "See, it's like being in a plane," I say, "circling the city."

We walk around the deck, and as we pass the elevator, I try to distract him by pointing to the Upper West Side and saying, "Hey, look, you can see my house from here." We circle again.

As the time gets closer to the last off-peak train, neither of us makes a move to leave. He points toward Brooklyn and says, "There's the Brooklyn Bridge. Your mother and I drove over that bridge on our first date."

My father and I have talked about my mother's illness and his loneliness, and even a little about their marriage, but never about their courtship. He continues:

Yeah, we were going to the Strand to hear Eddie Duchin. Your mother had this big straw hat, which she never put on. I remember it next to her on the seat as we went over the bridge, she held on to the brim. Bridges scared the hell out of her. I didn't know it then. Turned out her sister forced that silly hat on her, which she couldn't bring herself to wear and would be stuck carrying all night.

My poor mother: feeling her chest constrict as they drove over the Brooklyn Bridge, unable to share her panic on a first date, knowing that the bridge would have to be crossed again. Then I remember my mother telling me about the time they were driving home from Manhattan and got caught in a traffic gridlock as they were about to enter the Midtown Tunnel. My father had a panic attack (though he didn't know what to call it) and left the car. He scurried through the stalled traffic and my mother drove home alone. An hour after she got home, he showed up, having taken the Long Island Rail Road.

She was also going out with my friend Sam Hoffman, and she couldn't choose so she stopped seeing both of us. One day I saw her on the street and she looks at me and says, "I made a mistake."

That was it. That was the rest of my life.

I realize I couldn't have planned a better way to get my father to talk to me; silence is the path to the elevator. I ply him with questions about his bank-robber father, the club he belonged to as a teenager, his cross-country trip on the cusp of World War II, the bar he owned. My head overloads with material I want to remember.

Your grandfather was in Sing Sing when I was little, but when I went to visit they told me it was the "hospital." Later it was "college." By the time I was ten, I knew where he was. By that time I was taking care of myself and your grandmother.

The dog—Scrappy—got into some chicken bones and we took him to the vet, who pronounced him fine. When I came home from school the next day, the dog was dead. I carried him seven blocks and buried him in the park so your grandmother wouldn't see him.

Yeah, visiting your father in prison—it wasn't your norm. I was always ashamed of the whole bit. But remember now, even though they did have weapons on them, it was the gentleman's part of the industry. They were the clean men of the business: You never robbed anybody personally. It was not homes; it was businesses that were covered by insurance. You didn't stick anybody up. They had a regular crew, then they'd pick up other guys as they needed them. You must see Asphalt Jungle—*that will show you how it was.*

The time they put in—it took a lot of surveillance and time, months could go into it before they did something. If they'd put all that planning and scheming and brains into something legit, they probably could have made more money.

One of your grandfather's scams involved a midget named Boots. He and Boots would go to a fancy bar in Manhattan and argue about the details of a race they were fixing, exactly how the midget would engineer his fellow jockeys. When someone got curious, they offered to share the fix in exchange for a few bucks.

He knew them all. Introduced me to Lepke once at Detention, just said, "Lepke, I want you to meet my son."

Once we're walking and he points out a nice-looking woman: "You see her, one of the best pickpockets in the business." The pay-off is, he comes home one day, he was riding the train, and he says, "You wouldn't believe it I had my wallet picked. I never knew it. I got taken." He couldn't get over it. "They got it and I don't know how." It always bothered him.

My father will want to stay up here for hours, filibustering with his life story. Looking down at the distant oval of Madison Square Garden (where once I got dizzy climbing up to seats in the top row), I feel a surge of panic. What if an overwhelming urge to jump comes over me? I've never been tempted before, but people have been known to snap, and that sounds sudden and unexpected.

Breathe. I put my hand on my stomach and start counting to myself. I feel better, almost giddy with my newfound skill, though embarrassed at my silly fear of snapping. Now that I think about it—I would have to snap badly enough to climb the spiked fence without coming to my senses. I confront Madison Square Garden below as if staring down a bully.

"Tell me about East New York when you were growing up."

Oh, I can picture them all:

There was Lenny—he'd sit on the stoop all evening and late into the night during the summer because his hay fever was so bad and his wheezing and sneezing drove everyone nuts. He could sing and finally got in with the crowd by singing tenor on the street corner. One of the other kids rode on the handlebar of Lenny's bicycle and a car ran into them. Lenny just got banged up, but the other kid was killed. Word got around that Lenny had a sneezing attack. From then on, whenever anyone from the dead kid's family saw Lenny, they'd spit on the ground near his feet.

And Tommy. He was eight pounds overweight for the navy, which was the safest service to join during the war. He went on a diet to lose the weight so he could enlist with the other guys, but they wouldn't take him. He tied one on and they went looking for him. He was sitting out on the curb in front of his old poolroom, he was just sitting in front of the poolroom at two a.m. He was drafted into the army three or four months later. The first time he went out on a mission . . . he never made it.

We started the club on Bradford Street, Fraternal Fellows. We had about sixteen kinds of cards made up. Joe was in the club; my friend Nicky from Glenmore Avenue days; Sam Hoffman—the one who used to go with Mommy. We had this guy we called Big Boy. And there was a guy we called Mr. Tops—he used to stand out in the middle of the street and just start to spin around. Mishegas. Like your Uncle Jim, who collected keys, he was always asking for your old keys. Then he'd go to a dance or something and give them to the bandleader— "Hey,

I found these." The bandleader would hold them up and ask who lost them. We'd all laugh at everyone checking their pockets.

Hesh was a short little rotund guy who found it very difficult to get girls to go out with him—not that he didn't love to go out with the girls—so one time they pulled a cruel trick on him. He hears all this moaning from the back room, and they told him they had a girl in there and he's next. When he goes in, there are two of the guys simulating. If he had a gun he would have killed everybody. One time there was a girl in the crowd that put out. Everybody else knew her as the sweet little thing but she would go with a crowd of guys, no money, she just did it for the love of doing it. She said, "There's only one guy I won't put out for. Hesh."

Right around the corner, belonging to another club, was this fighter called Bummy Davis—you could look him up. They also had a guy who went to Hollywood and became a big-shot producer. He used to play poker with us. One night, he had four of a kind and the pot kept getting bigger. I had a straight flush. I don't care how much money he's made in Hollywood, I bet you he still remembers that hand.

In 1940 my father and a friend from the club bought a car and drove cross country. He was nineteen. I ask him how it happened.

Just talking, kid-talk, you sat around and did a lot of dreaming: one day we're gonna go. And we did it. We took off. We had a big eighty or ninety dollars. We paid about thirty-five dollars for the car. The very first night we got to Blairsville, Pennsylvania, and slept in the car along the side of the road.

We stayed with relatives in Chicago, and the Y in Reno, Salt Lake City, Hollywood. We got lots of autographs: Mary Astor, George Raft, Rosalind Russell, Greer Garson, Robert Young, Eddie Albert, Freddie Bartholomew.

One of the gang back home made this giant map of the US and put it on the wall at Jack's bicycle shop. They pinned our postcards on the places we sent them from, and everyone came by and checked on our progress. Forty years later I run into a guy at the track who recognized me from the old neighborhood. He remembered the map. We were gears back then.

It is getting cold, and my father says, "Let's go inside." A guy has a machine that flattens pennies into Empire State Building souvenirs. It costs a dollar, and, despite the price, my father lets me buy one for each of us without saying, "Nah, I got one yesterday." He insists on supplying the pennies. The guy punches holes in them, and we add them to our key chains. I ask about the bar he owned right after he got married.

The Montauk Tavern. My partner was Bright Eyes, we got the money from my father. Bright Eyes was always taking his pulse while looking at his watch, feeling his chest. Hypochondriac, always thought he was going to die.

"What happened to him?"

He died of a heart attack.

We both laugh.

We had a free lunch counter on the horseshoe bar. Ferranti was a drunken chef with a handlebar moustache who couldn't hold a job but made the best sauce you ever tasted. We let him sleep in the back and threw him three pennies each day to buy Il Progresso. *This Irish guy Brady was always the first customer on Saturday morning. Never saw him any other time.*

One New Year's Eve we wanted to stay open past three a.m., and your grandfather told me I had to go to the precinct, give the captain an envelope with a Christmas present. I get in to see the captain, tell him the name of the bar, and put the envelope on the table: "A little something for your family." He stares at me, cold, and says, "Son, if that's what I think it is you better just pick it up and walk away." I could have crawled out.

A week later he comes into the bar, I'm afraid to even offer him a free drink. He says he's been thinking, that it's not fair to his children if I want to do something for them, and asks if the envelope still has his name on it. I never even opened it. I give it to him and he wishes me a Merry Christmas, adjusts his hat, and leaves. Your grandfather comes in a couple of minutes later and says, "What was the old captain doing here?" "What do you mean old captain?" "He got transferred some-place up in the Bronx."

Always through the years, there were your grandfather's cronies come to the house and hung around. Charlie Irish, Blackie (a ladies' man, I don't know who passed him up, an enforcer, very deadly—you've got to have persuaders in every business, that was the game and when you got into the game you knew that was the price you had to pay), Dummy Taylor (I remember him cleaning fish), Big Joe the Pollock, Georgie Kalivas had a pushed-in nose. Pete Koback—he did a lot of jobs with your grandfather. He might have even been your godfather—who held you that day, who held you? There was Abe from the Garment District, if you had a problem he'd say, "Okay, I'll take care of it." Quiet, nat-tily dressed, heavyset man, not fat, big in stature, very impressive, spoke very softly. We had lunch at one of those side restaurants, and the red carpet was dragged out for him.

I tell him how exciting this all is to me.

There were some rough times. Your grandfather was away once and he left money behind. Your grandmother was seeing one of his cronies. When he got out he found out about it and the money was gone. He went into a rage and the result was she tried to kill herself. Took some pills. I got worried about her and went to the apartment but it was locked and I didn't have the key. I just started trying every key I had and one of them fit and I got her to the hospital. I still don't know how that happened, how I had a key that fit.

I used to see him do something that I never knew what he was doing. Maybe at that time it was a form of a drug. He used a little burner. I don't know what you do when you burn something. He used to do that in the bedroom. He did drink more than your average. He could hold it. He always had a bottle. He was always taking a shot.

The FBI came by after we got married—you know the kind, government men, business types with the shirts and ties like they just got out of college. They showed me pictures. I knew every picture. But I was very vague with my answers. When I had the milk route they came to the place and the boss says, "Hey, Matt, they were asking questions about you."

I remember one horrible snowstorm when he had the milk route and he didn't come home till late the next night.

It might have been '58. They predicted a big storm so I left the house at eleven p.m. It took me until seven in the morning to get to the place, load a truck, and get near the route. Nothing is plowed, everything is knee-high. Cars and trucks stuck. I stop at a little restaurant—a diner-type place—the Phoenix. What am I gonna do now? Kid sits next to me and he's having coffee. "You wanna make ten bucks," I ask and he says, "Yeah, doing what?" "Help me out delivering milk." "Okay, c'mon, let's go."

I had to work out of sequence of what I would normally do. This kid was good. We split up on each block. I rang the customers' bells so they'll know the milk is out there. They said, "What the hell are you doing here, are you crazy?" We got three-quarters of the way through, and it's seven o'clock at night. We stopped for doughnuts and coffee and ate in the truck. I told him, "Take as much milk as you can carry."

I walked in the house it was eleven p.m.—twenty-four hours straight, and I'm talking work, walking knee-deep in snow with a case of milk, running up flights of stairs palming two bottles in each hand. *I had to pay for all the milk, so I probably didn't make anything.*

"Why did you do it?"

Why did I do it? Why do you climb the mountain?

Rush hour has come and gone. Through the dark, amid the glitter, are the places my father has been talking about.

I guess I've been yapping a lot.

I remind him that when I used to come home for the weekend from college he hardly said a word to me.

I have a confession. I used to wish you wouldn't come home because I'd feel so empty when you left. On Sunday, I'd sit in the living room, by the window, as the sun went down and you got farther away. Your mother would say, "Why don't you put the light on?"

We finally enter the elevator. Again we get pressed to the back. We stare at the 20, waiting for it to glow as if searching for a beacon. It feels like the elevator really has stalled this time. "Uh-oh," a Japanese tourist says, and his companions laugh.

I avoid my father's eyes, not wanting to witness his moment of panic, but *I* panic, unable to flee, afraid I will faint (though I have never fainted). I start doing my deep breathing but can't break the cycle. I imagine myself screaming and my father screaming and the tourists laughing.

Out of the corner of my eye I see my father's hand on his stomach, moving slowly up and down, his lips moving slightly with the count.

The light for the twentieth floor comes on. We've been moving all along.

As we get out of the elevator, my father says:

That kid from the snowstorm—he's probably still telling that story.

About the Author

ERIN LANGSTON

Alan Ziegler's books include *The Swan Song of Vaudeville: Tales and Takes; The Green Grass of Flatbush* (stories); *So Much to Do* (poems); *Planning Escape* (poems); *The Writing Workshop*, volumes 1 and 2; and *The Writing Workshop Note Book: Notes on Creating and Workshopping*. He is editing *The Short Course: An International Anthology of Prose Poems, Brief Stories, and Other Shorts* for Persea Books, and he is at work on *Based on a True Life: A Memoir in Pieces*. His work has also appeared in such places as *Narrative, The New Yorker, The Paris Review, Tin House, American Poetry Review, Carolina Quarterly, The International Literary Quarterly*, and *Creative Writing in America*. Ziegler is a professor of writing and director of pedagogy at Columbia University's School of the Arts, where he was chair of the Writing Program from 2001 to 2006 and won the Presidential Award for Outstanding Teaching. He lives in New York City with his wife, Erin Langston.

We hope you enjoyed Alan Ziegler's *Love at First Sight*.

Please visit us at NARRATIVEMAGAZINE.COM
for more Narrative Library books.

13660976R00104

Made in the USA
Lexington, KY
13 February 2012